ALASKAN CHRISTMAS TARGET

SHARON DUNN

LOVE INSPIRED SUSPENSE
INSPIRATIONAL ROMANCE

LOVE INSPIRED® SUSPENSE
INSPIRATIONAL ROMANCE

ISBN-13: 978-1-335-40323-0

Recycling programs for this product may not exist in your area.

Alaskan Christmas Target

This edition published by arrangement with Harlequin Books S.A.

For questions and comments about the quality of this book, please contact us at CustomerService@Harlequin.com.

Love Inspired
22 Adelaide St. West, 40th Floor
Toronto, Ontario M5H 4E3, Canada
www.Harlequin.com

Printed in U.S.A.

Fear thou not; for I am with thee: be not dismayed;
for I am thy God: I will strengthen thee;
yea, I will help thee; yea, I will uphold thee
with the right hand of my righteousness.
—Isaiah 41:10

For my beautiful daughter Ariel.
Your creative spirit and sense of humor have brightened
my life and the tenacity of your character inspires me.

ONE

Natasha Hale watched through the window of the roadside diner where she worked as Gary Tharp pulled into the lot, parked crookedly and slammed on the brakes.

Feeling a rising panic, Natasha placed a breakfast order in front of an older couple. Gary was the violent ex-husband of Judy whose mother, Betsy, owned the diner. He had caused trouble before. Mostly over the custody agreement of his and Judy's son Ezra. Gary pushed open the car door, got out and leaned against the vehicle to steady himself. It was clear he'd been drinking. The snow swirling softly around him stood in sharp contrast to the intensity of his anger evident even from a distance. His expression was like hardened granite, eyebrows drawn together. He swayed as he walked.

It was just Natasha and Betsy working this morning. The only patrons were the older couple who had told her they were tourists. Just like every other weekday morning, eight-year-old Ezra occupied a table in the diner. Betsy took care of Ezra every night so her daughter, a nurse, could work the graveyard shift at the hospital. In the hours when she needed to open up the diner and before Judy got off shift, Ezra sat at a booth eating his breakfast and reading or coloring.

Natasha tensed as she glanced at Ezra and then out the window again. Because of Gary's volatility brought on by addiction issues, the boy's father had been granted only supervised visits since the divorce. It looked like he was on the warpath.

Ezra's mom was Natasha's friend. She needed to keep the boy safe. In the months that she had worked at the diner, she had grown fond of Ezra. He was a quiet boy who seemed to think deeply about most things. She felt a connection to Ezra for a different reason. She had a nephew who was only a little older than Ezra whom she would probably never see again. For the last year, Natasha had been cut off from family because she'd been put into the witness protection program.

Natasha hurried over to Ezra, who had just taken a bite of his toast. "Why don't we go in the back and you can help Grandma?" She glanced out the window. Gary was only feet away from the door.

"I'm not done eating." Ezra set his toast down on the plate.

"Just for now." Natasha tried to keep her voice level even though her heart was racing. She clutched Ezra's elbow, gently trying to lift him up.

Too late. The bell above the door jingled.

Gary's words pelted Natasha's back like a hard rain as she tried to usher the boy into a back room. "What are you doing with my son, Natasha?"

Once given her new identity, Natasha had kept her first name, as did most people in the program.

Natasha spun around just as Ezra said, "Daddy," in a voice that was faint and filled with anguish.

Natasha squared her shoulders, hoping her voice didn't give away the level of fear she was trying to hide. "I'm sorry, Gary, but I think you need to leave."

The Christmas music spilling out of a radio in the kitchen went silent. Ezra's grandmother came around the counter, wiping her hands on her apron. "You heard what Natasha said, Gary. You need to go, or I'll call the police."

Gary pounded his chest. "He's my boy, too." His eyes were glassy, and he was leaning to one side.

Ezra slipped his hand in Natasha's, making a noise that was almost a whimper.

"That's it, Gary. I'm calling the police." Betsy stalked back toward the kitchen.

Gary reached inside his jacket and pulled out a handgun. "You stop right there, old lady. Nobody is going anywhere."

Betsy turned around slowly. The older couple gasped in unison and then sat paralyzed, their eyes filled with fear.

What felt a like a lifetime ago, Natasha had been a police officer in Boston. She'd dealt with people like Gary all the time, their anger fueled and intensified by whatever substance they'd taken.

Gary waved the gun. "Ezra, come here."

"Gary, put the gun down." Natasha held her palm out toward the enraged man. "You don't have to do this. It won't end well."

"This is none of your business." He lifted the gun and pointed it at Natasha's chest.

Her heart beat even faster. She took in a shallow, sharp breath. "Please, Gary."

Ezra let go of Natasha's hand and ran to his father. "Don't hurt Natasha. I'll go with you. I promise."

"No, Ezra." Natasha reached out to the boy as Gary's finger slipped on the trigger. She froze in place, staring at the man who could kill her.

Gary's attention suddenly turned toward Ezra's grandmother. He repositioned his aim and pulled the trigger, shooting the cell phone out Betsy's hand. Pieces of the phone slid across the linoleum. All the color drained from Betsy's face. Her hands were shaking.

The shot rang in Natasha's ears. She couldn't get a deep breath.

From the booth where they were sitting, the older couple scooted to the far side of the room, clutching each other.

"Daddy, please, I'll go with you." Ezra tugged on his father's coat.

"Gary, you're in no condition to drive. Put the gun down," Natasha said. She had to prevent him from leaving with the child.

Gary straightened his back and raised his chin. His eyes cleared for just a moment. "You're right. I'm in no condition to drive. You're coming with us." He once again pointed the gun at Natasha.

It wasn't the scenario she'd hoped for, but she might be able to protect Ezra. Maybe she could overpower Gary before they got into the car. She rushed over to Ezra and wrapped her arm around his back, squeezing his shoulders. "Don't touch him." Gary aimed the gun at the older couple and then at Betsy as he walked backward. "No calling the police or Natasha gets it. She's my insurance."

They walked through the parking lot to his car. Any hope of escape ended when Gary stopped at the driver's door and put the gun to her temple. "Get in behind the wheel." He then spoke to Ezra without looking at him. "Get in the backseat, son. Do as I say."

Natasha sat behind the wheel. Her whole body trembled. Gary kept the gun trained on her through the windshield as he hurried over to the passenger's side of the car. He yanked open the front door, still pointing the gun at her as he settled into his seat. He pulled the keys out of his front shirt pocket and tossed them at her.

"Now drive."

Her hands shook as she stuck the key in the ignition and twisted it. The car roared to life. She caught a quick look at Ezra in the backseat. It wasn't fear she saw in his eyes, but confusion. He was a helpless pawn in an ugly game. The boy wanted his father's love and approval.

She shifted into Reverse and turned the car around so it faced the highway. No cars went by. Little Bear, Alaska, the town where she lived, had a population of a couple thousand and, even then, it was spread out. The diner was a mile from what passed for downtown.

"Where are we going?" Natasha asked.

"You don't need to know. Take a right on to the highway. I'll tell you when to turn off."

As she pulled out onto the highway, she caught a glimpse of the diner. Flashing Christmas lights that framed the windows, but no people, were visible. Despite Gary's threat, she knew Ezra's grandmother would call the police to save her grandson. Natasha had left her cell phone in the break room. Betsy would know to look for it there since the older woman's phone had been destroyed.

Help would come for them. Still, she feared that Gary would carry out his threat and shoot her if law enforcement showed up.

Natasha took in a prayer-filled breath.

Maybe she would die here today, but she vowed to do everything in her power to see that Ezra was returned to the people who loved him.

Alaska state trooper Landon Defries let out a heavy breath as he passed the Christmas tree farm buzzing with activity. This would be his second Christmas without Maggie. He used to think that there was something sad about people who didn't want to celebrate holidays. But now, after the loss of his wife, he understood that sometimes facing a holiday alone only intensified the pain.

His radio glitched.

"Defries here. What's up, Angie?"

"We got a custodial kidnapping. Gary Tharp has taken Ezra and a hostage—that waitress that works down at the Kodiak Diner. Last seen turning off the highway onto River Road."

Landon's stomach twisted.

"I'm on it." He pressed the gas. Gary's old rattletrap of a car would be easy enough to spot.

"Suspect is armed and dangerous. Betsy says she's pretty sure he'd been drinking or something worse."

"I'm gonna need backup."

"On it," said the dispatcher.

Landon sped down the highway. He was only minutes away from the turnoff to River Road. He clicked his blinker. He wasn't sure what Gary had in mind by taking River Road. There were, Landon knew, at least three or four spur roads that ran off it. One would take Gary even higher into the mountains, another down to a harbor where bush planes and boats were docked. The other roads led to private residences.

He clenched his jaw and stared straight ahead. Gary had already managed to endanger his son and that quiet woman who worked at the diner. If Gary sought shelter in one of the homes, even more people would be in danger. The last thing Landon wanted was some sort of standoff.

He checked his sideview mirror. No sign of reinforcements.

Up ahead, he caught a glimpse of the back end of Gary's car right before it disappeared down a steep incline.

He clicked on his radio. "Angie, where's my backup?"

"Deb and Russ are on their way. Both of them were at least ten miles out on other calls. They will get there as fast as they can. It's the best I can do, Landon."

Actually, it was surprising that the other two officers assigned to this area had been that close. Because so much of Alaska was remote, rural troopers covered a huge amount of territory. There were no sheriffs in Alaska. Troopers were the key law enforcement.

Landon whizzed by snow-covered evergreens. "Thanks, Angie. I'll do what I can."

Landon sped up even more. He passed the first turnoff, which he knew led to a house only occupied part of the year. His unobstructed view of the road to the residence told him Gary hadn't taken that turn.

Landon remembered that, though he'd lost his license, Gary had training as a bush pilot. The harbor was the most likely place for him to go if he was planning some sort of escape.

He surged ahead.

Gary's car came into view and it looked like the waitress was behind the wheel, with Gary right next to her. Ezra's head barely came above the rim of the back window.

Landon's heart squeezed tight.

God, don't let anything bad happen to that kid or that woman.

TWO

The barrel of the gun dug into Natasha's stomach. Sweat trickled down her back. Being held at gunpoint brought back bad memories from her days as a police officer.

Gary glanced nervously over his shoulder. "Go faster."

"I'm going as fast as this thing will go. I've got the pedal to the floor."

The trooper was maybe four car lengths behind them.

"We got to lose this guy. Slow down, let him get a little closer."

What exactly did Gary have in mind?

He put the gun against her temple. "I said, slow down."

"Okay. Okay." She let up on the gas.

Gary rolled down his window, stuck his head and arm out and took aim at the trooper.

Natasha sped up just as he fired two shots. Behind her, the trooper's vehicle slowed. It looked like his windshield had been shattered. Had the trooper been hit?

Gary spoke through gritted teeth. *"Slow down."*

"I'm sorry. I… I just panicked."

"You knew exactly what you were doing," he shouted at her and then glanced over his shoulder.

The trooper's car was still rolling toward them. Gary stuck his head out the window again and fired off more shots. "That should do it. Now speed up."

This time she did as she was told.

The trooper's patrol car grew smaller in her rearview mirror. The vehicle hadn't veered off the road and crashed. Maybe, she thought, he was still alive. The car looked like it was barely moving as steam rolled out from under the hood. The last shots had probably damaged the engine.

"There's a little gravel road up ahead on the right that dead ends. Turn off there," Gary said. "We have to fool him. He can still see where we're going."

"Daddy." Ezra's voice sounded small and faraway. The boy was hunched with his arms crossed over his chest. "What's happening?"

Only Ezra's voice seemed to change Gary's threatening demeanor. His shoulders slumped a little, and the pressure of the gun against her skin lessoned.

"It's going to be okay, son. You and I are going to have an adventure. Remember when you used to go up in the plane with Daddy?" Gary's voice took on a gentle, almost vulnerable quality.

Ezra lifted his head a little. "Yes, I remember."

They bounced along on the gravel road. She stopped the car when they came to a rock outcropping in the middle of the road. Beyond that, the trees and brush grew so thick that the road disappeared entirely. "Why are we stopping here?"

"Ezra, get out of the car and wait for me," Gary said.

From the backseat, the boy pushed the passenger-side door open.

Gary leaned close to her and spoke in her ear. "You are my insurance policy. Even if we stopped that one cop, I'm sure there will be more. Do as I say, and I'll let you go. We got off track because of that cop, but I have a way to get out of here." He tilted his head downhill in the direction of the harbor.

Gary was hard to read. He was so erratic. A minute ago, he'd threatened her life. She was beginning to wonder if it was just alcohol he was under the influence of or something much more damaging to his decision-making skills. He didn't seem to understand the consequences of what he was doing, for himself and for his son.

As messed up as he was, he did seem to have a sort of plan. Did he have a plane or boat waiting for him at the harbor or was he just hoping to steal one?

"I'm going to get out first and then you can exit the car." He pulled the keys from the ignition. "Don't try anything."

"I'll do as you say, Gary." The best strategy seemed to be to appear cooperative and to look for a chance to escape with Ezra. "Just don't hurt Ezra."

"I would never do anything bad to my boy."

Gary had been so indignant, she dared not point out that kidnapping at gunpoint could be traumatizing to a child. The man was not thinking clearly—or not thinking at all.

Just go along with him until you have a chance to save yourself and the boy.

Even though Gary was armed, she had been a beat

cop in Boston. Though her skills were rusty, she'd had enough training to take down an armed felon. All she needed was an opportunity. She prayed for a moment of inattention or distraction. The tricky part would be getting Ezra to safety. The boy showed a loyalty to his father that might make him reluctant to leave him.

It wasn't a bond she understood, but she'd seen it a thousand times. Kids in safe foster homes who ran back to their abusive biological parents. The bond between parent and child was a hard one to break even when it was not healthy.

Gary stepped out of the car, keeping the gun trained on her the whole time. She peered through the passenger window, offering Ezra a faint smile as if to say, *I know this is so confusing to you.*

When the US Marshal had set her up in this town, he had advised her not to form strong bonds with anyone. Though she'd remained guarded and had not given up many details about her life, the friendship with Ezra's mom and Betsy had just happened. In the early morning hours when the diner was not usually busy, she brought Ezra his toast and sausage. It wasn't just that Ezra reminded her of the nephew she would never see again, she'd grown fond of his sweet nature.

Gary waved the gun, indicating that she needed to get out of the car. She pushed open the driver's-side door. Though she had on a sweater and long johns under jeans, the chilly December air permeated her skin.

Gary pointed with his free hand while he kept the gun aimed at Natasha. "Now we're going to head down that way." He indicated a path that wasn't really a trail. "Ezra, stay beside me." He looked directly at Natasha. "You walk ahead of me."

Natasha fell into place and headed down the hill. Within minutes, the harbor with its boats and planes came into view. Though still some distance off, it didn't look like anyone was around. Gary had made her walk in front so that if she could tried to run away, she'd have to leave Ezra behind. He must have known she wouldn't do that. And if she did start running, he could shoot her in the back before she found cover.

They entered a cluster of trees that obstructed her view of the harbor.

"We need to go faster," Gary said. "Pick up the pace."

She went from a brisk walk to a jog. She could hear Gary and Ezra's footsteps pounding behind her. Her breath came out in puffy clouds. The trees cleared and she had an unobstructed view of the harbor once again. Still no sign of anyone. It was a small harbor. Two planes, a fishing boat and two recreational boats.

"Dad, I can't keep up. I need to catch my breath."

"We're almost there, son." Gary was a little out of breath, too.

She glanced over her shoulder as she slowed down. Gary still had the gun pointed at her. As far as she could see, there was no one else in the harbor. No one anywhere. Gary had taken them on a small detour. Would the trooper be able to make it here on foot if he was not injured? Was he even alive?

A light snow swirled out of the sky as they stepped on the wooden planks of the pier, which had some icy patches.

Gary cupped his son's arm. "You see that plane over there? That is our plane. You remember how I taught you to start a plane?"

Ezra nodded.

"I need you to go do that for me. And then I want you to sit in the copilot seat and wait for me, you hear?"

Fear gripped Natasha's heart. What did Gary have in mind to do with her?

"Okay, Dad." Ezra walked toward the plane. He gave a backward glance, locking eyes with Natasha.

She saw the twisted anguish in the boy's expression. Maybe it was loyalty to his dad that made him do as he was asked and maybe it was fear of his father's anger. Most likely it was a mixture of both.

Gary stepped in between Natasha and Ezra so she couldn't make eye contact with the boy. "Go on now, son."

Gary turned his back to his son and drew his attention to her. The gun was still pointed at her chest. "I need you to turn your back toward me." His words were ice-cold.

A moment later, the propellers of the plane started to whir. With Ezra inside the plane, there was less possibility of him being be hurt. If Gary got on that plane, he could take Ezra and never be heard from again. This was her opportunity, her only chance to prevent that from happening.

"I said turn around and keep your hands up where I can see them."

Natasha did not move. She looked all around at the other boats and then at the forest close to the harbor. Help was not coming. It was up to her to protect Ezra, and it might come at the expense of her life.

She took in a prayer-filled breath and lunged at Gary. His finger covered the trigger, the gun barrel aimed at her chest.

* * *

Landon bolted from the trees. When his car would no longer run due to a bullet through the engine, he'd taken an educated guess that Gary would eventually show up at the harbor since the spur road he'd turned onto would not allow him to escape. Landon had run all the way there.

He had some distance to cover before he could get to the pier and he was out of breath already. He didn't see the boy anywhere. He watched in shock as the waitress from the diner took Gary down in two quick moves. A blow to the stomach, a kick to the back of the knees. The gun went off in the struggle though Gary lost his grip on it. He jumped to his feet and dove at the woman, preparing to put his hands around her neck. She angled out of his way before he could grab her. His hand formed a fist, and he punched her in the stomach. She doubled over. He turned to retrieve his gun.

Landon's feet crunched across the half-melted snow. He drew his weapon just as Gary was about to take aim at the waitress. "Alaska State Trooper. Back off from the lady and put your hands in the air. Drop the gun."

Gary seemed to know he was defeated. He lifted his hands in surrender letting the gun drop to the wooden pier.

The waitress dove for the gun. She had nerves of steel and quick reaction time. At the very least, she had some self-defense training. Though the woman had been in Little Bear at least a year, Landon really didn't know much about her. Any time he'd come into the diner, she'd seemed quiet and aloof.

The propeller on the plane stopped whirring.

Landon continued to advance, keeping the gun trained on Gary.

The window on the plane slid open. "Daddy, what's happening?"

Gary pressed his lips together, and his forehead furrowed. "It's okay, son."

"Ezra, stay in the plane," Natasha said.

"Am I going with my dad?"

"No, I think it would be better if you stayed with your mom and grandma. Besides, who is going to eat the last piece of peach pie with me on Sundays if you aren't there?"

"Hands behind your back." Landon moved in to cuff Gary.

Gary leaned toward Natasha. "This is all your fault. A father has a right to be with his son. You are going to pay." His words were filled with murderous rage.

Another trooper vehicle came into view as it rolled down the hill toward the pier. Trooper Deb Johnson got out. "Looks like I missed all the action."

"Not quite," Landon said. "Get this guy secured in the back of your vehicle."

Deb took Gary into custody.

Landon walked over to the plane to help Ezra out.

Clearly upset, Natasha paced the pier, running her hand through her long auburn hair. She finally turned and walked toward Landon and Ezra. "I really need to get back to the diner. I want to finish out my shift."

Once he had Ezra out of the plane, Landon put his hand on the boy's shoulder and gave it a reassuring squeeze. He then turned his attention to Natasha. "You've had quite a shock. Are you sure you want to go back to the diner?"

She nodded. "I need the money. I don't want to sit alone at home all tied up in knots." She offered Ezra a smile. Maybe part of her motivation for wanting to return to the diner was to make sure the boy was okay.

"I'll take you both back to the diner, but I don't want to transport you and Ezra in the same vehicle as Gary. There should be another trooper here in a few minutes."

"That's fine." Natasha nodded and shifted her focus to Ezra. "I know this is so confusing for you. We'll get you back to your mom and grandma. They'll be so happy."

The boy let out a small cry and then ran toward Natasha, who took him into an embrace. She made soothing sounds while he cried.

Landon felt a stab to his own heart over all the child had been put through at such a young age.

The second trooper vehicle came down the road, pulling off to the side so the one transporting Gary could get up the hill.

"Come on, Ezra. I'll stay with you," Natasha said. She walked the boy toward the trooper vehicle, gripping his shoulder.

Landon kept pace with them, opening the back door so they could get inside. He got into the front passenger seat.

Russ, a man in his forties with graying sideburns, gave Landon a nod. "Sorry I couldn't be here for all the excitement."

Landon buckled his seat belt. "We handled it." He gave a nod toward Natasha, who seemed focused on making sure Ezra was okay. "I know you got here as fast as you could."

Russ pressed the gas and drove forward so he could turn around.

Natasha spoke in a soft voice to Ezra. "You'll be okay, kiddo. Grandma might even let you have one of her homemade doughnuts."

Ezra nodded. "I like grandma's doughnuts." His voice sounded like he might start crying again.

She brushed her hand over the top of his head. "I'm so sorry. I know it doesn't make sense…what happened here today."

"What's going to happen to my dad?" The boy's voice was filled with anguish.

Landon turned sideways as Natasha glanced in his direction.

"Your father needs some help," Landon told him. "I know you love him, but what he did today wasn't right."

They drove past Landon's defunct trooper car; he was going to have to arrange for a tow. Russ made his way back to the main road and drove for several miles, the rest of the journey consisting of small talk between him and Russ.

When they pulled into the parking lot of the diner, a news van was there. A female reporter and a cameraman were standing beside the van.

"What's with those guys?" Natasha asked. "How did they get here so fast?" She seemed even more nervous at seeing the news van.

"Guess they must have heard the banter on the police band radio," Russ said.

"They probably want to interview the citizen who helped save Ezra," Landon guessed.

"Me? No, I don't want to be on camera." She grew even more agitated.

With a glance at the news van, Natasha leaned toward Ezra. "Come on, let's get you back to your mom and grandma. They're going to be so glad to see you." She helped him out of the car.

Betsy and Judy came running out to embrace the boy. The crew filmed the reunion and then the female reporter stepped up to Natasha. The tall blonde pointed a microphone at her. "You must be the hero waitress who saved Ezra."

Natasha took a step back. "It really was the trooper's work."

"Going with the boy into such danger is pretty heroic," the reporter said. "What were you thinking?"

"I just didn't want Ezra to be hurt or kidnapped by his dad." Natasha turned her attention toward the cameraman. "I don't want to be filmed."

"This is a big story for a little town," the reporter said.

"Please, I don't want my face on camera." Natasha seemed to grow even more upset.

"This is a live feed. The story had already gone out," the reporter noted.

"You mean showing my face." Natasha seemed to be almost in a panic.

"Yes, we did an intro before you got here. The story will be all over social media. People want to hear your side of this story."

Natasha continued to shake her head.

The reporter gave the cameraman the signal to cut the camera. She turned to face Natasha. "You deserve some recognition. We would like to get a shot of all of you together, hugging, and I can do my wrap-up with that in the background."

Natasha stepped to one side. "You know, the real heroes here are our troopers. You should interview them." She turned and hurried inside the diner.

The female reporter looked at Russ and then at Landon. Landon pointed to Russ. "I'm sure he'd be glad to make a statement." He wasn't crazy about reporters, either, but this one had seemed to send Natasha into a tailspin.

The reporter held the microphone toward him. "But he wasn't the one who captured Gary Tharp. It was you and the waitress working together, right?"

He needed to get a statement from Natasha and wanted to find out why she was acting so strange. With the reporter trailing after him, he walked past the reunited family as they hugged and cried. Landon reached for the front door of the diner.

A car with Natasha at the wheel came around from the back, where the employees parked, and pulled out of the lot and sped down the highway.

Landon shook his head. She was sure in an all-fired hurry to leave after she'd insisted she needed to get back to the diner and finish her shift. Almost like she was afraid of something.

Something was definitely going on with her. Being filmed seemed to set her off. Most people didn't want to be on the news because they were hiding, maybe from an abusive partner or because they were in trouble with the law. He wondered which one it was with Natasha.

THREE

Natasha raced down the highway toward the little cabin that she'd rented for the last year. She hit her blinker and turned onto the side road that led to her cabin, which was tucked back in the trees, out of view. How long did she have before the mafia saw the news story and came after her? Hours? Days? Weeks? Maybe she was safe. Maybe she wasn't. She couldn't take that chance.

She grabbed her purse off the car seat, grateful to see that Betsy had put her phone back inside it. She hurried up the walkway, unlocked the front door and entered her living room. Her mind was racing. She pulled a suitcase out of a closet and carried it to her bedroom. While she tossed in clothes, she grabbed her phone and dialed a number she'd memorized.

It rang twice before someone picked up; a woman with a chipper-sounding voice. "Hello?"

Not what she expected. "I'm trying to reach US Marshal Henderson. This is still his contact number, isn't it?"

"The marshal is up north, dealing with a prisoner transport," the woman said.

Natasha took in a deep breath to quell the rising panic. "When will he be back?"

"Unknown. Can I pass on a message? He has limited phone service and arranged for all his calls to be forwarded to me until he gets back. I'm a US Marshal, as well."

"No, I need to speak directly to him."

Marshal Henderson had helped Natasha settle into her new life. She trusted him, but no one else. Her first placement with a new identity hadn't worked out because of a leak, the source of which was never discovered. The mafia had snitches in all branches of law enforcement. She had to be careful. She had no idea who this woman was.

She'd been put in the witness security program after witnessing a mafia boss kill a politician. The murder had occurred in a secluded garden where a fundraiser was taking place. Leo Tan Creti, the mafia boss, usually hired out his dirty work. Strangling the DA who was trying to clean up the city had been a crime of opportunity for Leo. He hadn't counted on Natasha being a witness.

The woman's voice brought Natasha back to the present reality of how vulnerable she was. "Is there something I can do to help you? If you are in danger, we need to address that."

Because the mafia had such long arms which extended into law enforcement, she wasn't sure who she could trust. Police departments had corrupt cops and cops that could be bought, as did federal agencies. After her testimony had sent Leo away, a bounty had been put on her head. Leo Tan Creti could give orders from a jail cell almost as easily as when he was on the street. She placed her hand over her racing heart. Marshal Henderson was the only one she trusted. "There is no way to reach him?"

"Like I said, cell service is sketchy up there. He'll check in when he can. Are you sure there is not anything I can tell him?" The woman sounded concerned.

"No, thank you. I'll try back later."

Natasha hung up and threw more things in her suitcase. She would need to ditch this phone. The number might be traceable. She had three throw-away phones stored in a drawer. She tossed those into her suitcase. She'd been prepared for this day from the moment Henderson had set her up in her new life.

Normally with WITSEC, a member of local law enforcement would be informed of a participant's status. Marshal Henderson had advised against it in Natasha's case because Little Bear was such a small community. There was too much danger of an officer becoming loose lipped after drinking too much, he'd said, or just spilling the beans for whatever reason.

She stopped for a moment and stared at what she'd placed in her suitcase. The three burner phones sat on top of her sweaters and other cold-weather gear, and some random clothes. She'd been in full-on frantic mode ever since the cameraman had pointed the news camera at her. She needed to be rational and come up with a plan. She could drive to Anchorage and hide out until Marshal Henderson got back.

Natasha sat on the end of the bed and took a deep breath to shake off the tightness in her chest, a physical response to how alone she was. Disconnected from friends and family. No one to go to for help. This sense of isolation had happened once before. After her husband had been shot in the line of duty five years ago she found herself freefalling in shock and grief, forgotten by the world. But then her sister and other police officers had stepped into the gap after Jay's death. Now she had no one. No one but God.

If this last year had held a single blessing, it was that she had learned a deeper dependence on God. She closed her eyes and prayed.

God, I need Your help. Tell me what to do.

The answer came almost immediately. She needed to assess the reach of a regional news story posted on social media. She ran into the kitchen to get her laptop. Once on Facebook, she typed in the call letters of the news station. The story about Ezra came up first: Hero Waitress Saves Little Boy.

Her throat constricted as she watched. The reporter stood outside the diner, saying they were waiting for the little boy and the hero waitress. There was footage of her filmed at a distance as she helped Ezra out of the trooper's car. And then there was the footage of the reporter asking her questions. Her face was clearly visible.

She had to assume that their search for her was far-reaching and constant.

Natasha hurried back to the bedroom and threw a few more things into her suitcase. For tonight, she'd get out of Little Bear. She'd be more anonymous in Anchorage. She'd stay at a hotel or an out-of-the-way cabin and pay cash. Setting her coat on the bed, she grabbed the envelope of money she'd saved and stuffed it into the pocket.

She then went back to the kitchen and rifled through cupboards for food, grabbing protein bars and other items that had a long shelf life. She'd kept plenty on hand. For the last year, her life had been set up for this just-in-case scenario. One where she would be on the run.

Natasha reached into the depths of a drawer where she kept a sheathed hunting knife. She wished she had a gun. But buying one would have required a background check and registration, or getting it illegally, both of which could have put her back on the radar. She tossed the knife on top of the food she'd gathered into a box.

Finally, Natasha hurried out to her car and shoved the box of food onto the backseat. Though it had stopped snowing, the winter chill sunk into her skin. She put the knife in the glove box and hurried back to get her coat and her suitcase.

After putting on an extra layer of clothing and grabbing her down coat, she lifted the suitcase. As she walked through the living room, her gaze rested on the Christmas decorations she'd set up.

A year ago, she had had only hours to decide if she wanted to be in WITSEC. They'd kept her at a safe house until she could testify at trial and then set her up with a new identity in a different part of the world. She picked up one of the few personal items she'd taken with her: a wooden nativity that fit in the palm of her hand. It was a single piece, not more than five inches in length, depicting Jesus lying in the manger and Mary and Joseph looking down on their newborn child. Her grandfather had carved it. She grabbed it now and put it in her coat pocket.

Natasha took one more look at the cozy cabin that had been her home for the last year. A flash of movement in her peripheral vision caught her attention. She whirled around to look through the window that faced the backyard, which was forest. Her heart pounded as she stepped closer to the window, studying the trees and the spaces in between. It was possible that a deer or other wildlife had veered close to her house.

She took in a breath. She shook her head. Was it possible the mafia had sent an assassin that quickly?

Still, she felt a sense of urgency. She couldn't stay here any longer. It was too risky. She hurried out the front door, locking it behind her and then placing the keys under the mat where the owner would find them.

She ran out to the car, yanked open the back door and tossed her suitcase onto the seat. Her attention was suddenly drawn toward the front tire on the driver's side. It was flat. She knelt to look a little closer. Her hand touched the uneven surface as fear seized her. The tire had been punctured.

Natasha shook her head. This was not happening. It couldn't be. How could they get to her so fast? She hurried around to the other side of the car. Both front tires were flat. She needed to get out of here right now. It was at least half a mile to the main road.

She glanced around as she moved toward the backseat where she'd tossed her suitcase. Whoever had slashed her tires must have parked somewhere down the road and hiked to her house. They were probably hiding in the trees, waiting for the opportune moment to jump her or to shoot her from a distance.

She flung open the suitcase and dug for one of the burner phones.

She needed to call someone for help; at least to get a ride to a bus station. She would have to make up some kind of story. Judy and Betsy had been through enough today, but there was no one else.

She thought of the trooper who had spoken so kindly to her and to Ezra. Would he see through her story? Could she trust him with her secret?

She'd be less of a target in the cabin, where she could lock the doors and wait for help. After shutting the car door as quietly as possible, she hurried back to the cabin.

The forest that surrounded her house remained quiet. How strange. This wasn't the usual mafia MO. Their style was to be quick and efficient. If possible, they would shoot at a distance and leave or come in close to for the kill then disappear without a trace.

Natasha glanced side to side as she headed for the front door. She bent over to get the key from underneath the welcome mat. She straightened and inserted the key in the keyhole.

A hand went over her mouth.

"No one comes between me and my boy."

Gary Tharp. Somehow, he must've escaped. She elbowed him in the stomach, whirled around and karate chopped the nerve in his neck. The move stunned him. She turned, reaching for the doorknob. If she could get inside and lock the door, she'd have time to call for help.

He grabbed her from behind, pulling her hair. Natasha pivoted and swung at him but could not make contact before he yanked her forward by the collar. She'd dropped the phone in the snow at the side of the walkway. He pulled her face closer to his. The bloodshot eyes, the wild eyed expression, all of it communicated that he was high on something and bent on violence.

She punched him in the stomach and slapped him across the face. The move was enough to delay his reaction.

She headed toward the forest. She had to get away from him. Maybe double back and get to the safety of the house. It was clear his rage and whatever substance he had consumed would drive him to kill her.

Landon hit the turn signal on his truck and headed for the road that led to Natasha's cabin. Half an hour ago, Gary Tharp had escaped custody on the drive to jail. Trooper Deb Johnson had suffered minor injuries.

The assumption was that Gary would return for Ezra again. Deputies had been dispatched immediately to Ezra's house. So far, Gary hadn't showed up there. Landon was already off duty and on his way to his house when Russ had called him with the news.

Remembering the threat Gary had made against Natasha, he thought he'd better call her to warn her. He'd gotten her number from Betsy. When she hadn't answered her phone, he'd decided it would be best to check on her. At the very least, she needed to know Gary was no longer in custody. He also wanted to find out a little more about why she had been so upset about the news crew filming her.

A short distance from the cabin, he spotted the car Gary was reported to have stolen. He stopped and jumped out of his truck. A quick examination told him Gary wasn't in the car. He'd parked it off to the side, so it wouldn't be visible from the cabin. Landon ran back to his own vehicle, pressing on the gas as he closed the door. He clicked into his seat belt and accelerated. The road was icy. His truck slid but he maintained control.

He rounded a curve and caught sight of the cabin with Natasha's car parked in front.

He pulled his phone out. "Russ, I'm going to need some backup over at Natasha Hale's house. The car Gary stole is just down the road."

"On it," Russ said.

He came to stop by Natasha's car and kept talking into the phone. "It looks like Natasha's front tires have been slashed. I'm going to search the house and the area around it… Don't argue with me. I'm willing to take the risk. We could be out of time by the time another trooper can get here."

Procedure was to wait for backup, but Landon had the gut feeling he didn't have that option. Waiting was not a good idea if he wanted to keep Natasha alive.

He clicked his phone off and pushed open the truck door, thinking that if he had still been on duty, he would have had a gun with him. He circled her car and peered in a window. He furrowed his brow. A suitcase was flung open on the backseat with two throw-away phones on top of some clothes. He pulled open the door to examine the box beside it, which held winter gear and food.

He shook his head. None of this made any sense. It looked like Natasha was preparing to leave town, permanently or for a short break, he could only speculate. Two disposable phones was a little weird.

He turned his attention to the cabin's front door. The key was in the lock, as if someone, probably Natasha, had gone to open the door and been stopped. He found another disposable phone in the snow beside the walkway. Why would she have three burner phones? He had a feeling Natasha was not who she said she was.

The footprints around the door were too abundant to tell any kind of a story. When he saw footprints leading around the side of the cabin, he took off running.

The prints indicated two people running, one chasing the other. It was easy enough to speculate at what had gone down. Feeling a rising sense of urgency, Landon followed the trail to where it led into the trees. Once the canopy of the forest shielded the ground from snow, the footprints disappeared. He turned one way and then the other as his heart pounded in his chest. Though there were no longer any distinct footprints, he could only assume that Natasha had taken the path of least resistance through the open areas in the forest.

He pulled out his phone and pressed in Russ's number. "It looks like Gary chased Natasha into the trees behind her cabin."

"I'm on my way there now," Russ told him. "I still got an ETA of about twenty minutes. Deb is out of commission due to the injuries she sustained trying to keep Gary in custody. She is keeping an eye on Ezra at his school."

That was the biggest issue with living in sparsely populated parts of the world. The troopers had such large territories to cover and such limited help that when something like this did happen, they were often alone in the fight.

"This can't wait." Landon burst into a sprint. "I'm going to keep looking for them." He clicked off his phone while he ran, shoving it into his shirt pocket.

Landon hurried through the trees scanning side to side for any sign that Gary and Natasha might have come this way. When the trees opened up, he found two sets of footprints. One over the top of the other, which meant that Natasha was probably still on the run. Gary hadn't caught her yet.

He kept running in the direction the footprints indicated, finding more footprints that looked fresh. The forest opened up to a meadow. The recently fallen snow revealed the path the two people had gone. He caught a flash of color and movement on the other side of the open area. Someone had just disappeared into the trees across the meadow. He was getting closer.

He prayed he would reach Natasha in time to keep Gary from hurting her. Landon took in a deep breath. His exhale formed a cloud. It was getting colder.

He jogged across the meadow. The hours he spent at the gym and running the hills meant it would be a long time before he tired. Since Maggie's death, exercising and working were the only things that had kept him from giving in to despair.

He entered the trees on the other side of the meadow and stopped to listen. A breeze rustled the branches, but other than that, silence seemed to surround him.

Then he heard a woman scream.

FOUR

Natasha screamed as she tumbled down the steep incline. Not much snow had settled on the windswept mountainside. She banged against rocks and dirt. A moment earlier, Gary had lunged at her. To escape his grasp, she'd stepped back and the ground had given way.

She came to a stop on a flat spot. Her body felt like it had been beaten with boards. She'd be bruised for certain, but there was no immediate pain to indicate anything was broken. She hadn't hit her head on the way down. When she looked up, Gary was staring down at her, his features drawn into a sinister grimace.

Fear encroached on her thoughts. Just what did he have in mind? She'd fallen at least thirty feet. The rest of the way, to where the land flattened out and connected with a river, was steep. Only a climber with gear could hope to make it down such a perilous incline.

She scanned the rocks above her. She might be able to climb up, but Gary would be waiting there.

Gary's head disappeared from view.

He wouldn't have just left. She was in a very vulnerable place. He had something in mind. The ledge she'd landed on was only a little over a foot wide.

Gary peered over the edge of the incline. He grinned. He was holding a large rock. He let go of it. The rock hurtled toward her. She moved to the side as it crashed on the ledge and then rolled along the remainder of the steep incline.

A moment later, another rock was coming at her. She jerked to get out of the way, slipping off the ledge and rolling. She reached out, finding a protruding rock. She held on and looked up.

Gary had another rock raised above his head. She braced. He was probably aiming for her hands so the pain of impact would make her let go and fall to her death.

She closed her eyes and breathed a wordless prayer, then glanced back up.

Gary looked to the side, suddenly dropped his rock and took off running.

What in the world?

A moment later, Trooper Landon Defries's head appeared.

She'd never been so happy in her life.

"Can you hang on? It's too steep for me to get down to you. Search and rescue will be able to get you out with the chopper."

Her hands were tiring from holding on. Already her grip was loosening. "I can't hang on much longer."

Landon glanced in the direction Gary must have run then turned his attention back to her.

"Off to your right and up about a foot. There's a rock that is sticking out. Do you see it?"

She craned her neck. "Yes, I see it."

"That is a more secure place to wait. Do you think you can get up there?"

Her arms were weakening from the strain of holding on. "I'll try."

Again, he looked over his shoulder. He must be weighing his options. As a lawman, he was probably concerned about capturing Gary. He knelt and leaned over the incline. "I'll stay with you until help can come. I need to phone search and rescue." Landon had made a hard choice between chasing down Gary and making sure she was safe.

"Okay." She wasn't sure if she could reach the more secure position on the mountain.

He must have picked up on the fear in her voice.

He bent his neck as he stared down at her. "About three feet to the right below you, it looks like there is a foothold."

When she looked down, all she saw was the rocky shore that surrounded the river. Nausea overtook her.

"Natasha, I need you to focus."

"I know." She was weak from her flight from Gary. Her hands strained as she clung to the rock.

Landon stood. "Give me a second." He disappeared.

She could hear the rush of the river beneath her. She prayed she would be able to hang on.

Landon reappeared holding a tree branch. "I won't be able to get all the way down to you, but I'm going to help pull you up to that ledge." He moved a few feet down the mountainside, seeking a secure place to stand. He slipped. Rocks rolled past her, tumbling and crashing into each other.

Her heart skipped a beat. "Careful." Her voice sounded faint and faraway. Both of them didn't need to fall to their death today.

Landon edged a few feet down and then extended

the tree branch in her direction. "You're going to have to grab hold. Let go of the rock one hand at a time."

An exercise in trust. Something she had very little of after all that had happened. She looked up at Landon, who locked her in his gaze and nodded. He shook the tree branch.

"Once you have the branch. You should be able to gain a foothold beneath you. I see an outcropping below you that looks pretty solid."

She nodded, but inside her stomach was doing a gymnastics routine. She reached a hand out for the branch, grabbing hold while her legs flailed. Her feet found the outcropping. She let go of the rock with her other hand and gripped the branch. She took in a sharp, quick breath.

"I got you," he said.

Now she could see the clear path to the ledge Landon had pointed out. "I think I can make it." It was maybe five feet of climbing, some of it sideways.

She let go of the branch and reached up, her arm stretched as far as it could, muscles straining. She lifted one foot and felt around until her boot touched solid ground.

Landon held on to the branch and remained on his ledge. "I got to call this in to get help."

"I understand." She spoke through gritted teeth as she pulled herself up another six inches, finding a handhold and firm ground for her foot off to the side.

Landon made two calls. One to search and rescue, and another to Russ advising him of where Gary had last been seen.

Natasha pulled herself up to the wider ledge. The

exertion had left her breathless. He was at least twenty feet above her and ten feet from the top of the mountain.

She listened to the steadiness of his voice while she caught her breath.

He hung up. "Search and rescue is on the way with a chopper."

"Sounds good," she said. "Thanks for literally talking me off my ledge. I know you probably wanted to catch Gary."

"A trooper has been sent to watch the car Gary stole and parked not too far from your place. Gary might try to get back to it. We'll be able to do an air search of the forest with the chopper once you're safe."

"I hope he doesn't get away, for Ezra's sake."

Landon let out a heavy breath and shook his head. "Lot of places in this part of the world a man can hide. We'll catch him sooner or later."

The wind kicked up and she pressed a little closer to the mountainside. "I guess we have nothing to do but wait now."

Landon nodded. He put his phone away and then zipped his coat up tighter around his neck. He looked out into the distance and then back at her. "So, from the contents of your car, it looked like you were planning on going somewhere before Gary slashed your tires." He lifted his chin. "You seemed to be in a big hurry when you left the diner." A note of confrontation colored his words.

Her throat constricted from fear. She didn't know much about Landon. He came into the diner from time to time, but never talked much. She knew his wife had died and that he had a reputation as a good trooper. Back in Boston, she had trusted cops who'd ended up being dirty or on the take. One had even tried to kill her before the trial. The adage that you couldn't judge a book by its cover or man by the uniform was true. Her life depended on not trusting anyone. "I was headed out to see some family for the holidays."

"Oh really, where at?"

She was rusty, but she could read his body language and the inflection of his voice well enough to know that he didn't believe her...and she didn't trust him.

"Just up north." Best to divert him from his train of thought with a question. "How about you, you got a big Christmas planned?"

His posture stiffened as he squared his shoulders and glanced off to the side. "I got family around. Just don't care much for celebrating anymore."

Pain permeated his words and stabbed at her heart. She wanted to tell him that she understood more so than most people. She'd lost her own husband after they'd been married only a couple of years. But that was her old life. The life no one could find out about. "I'm sorry about your wife. Betsy told me."

He nodded, then a long silence fell between them, which made it clear he didn't want to talk anymore. He walked away and then returned. At least ten minutes passed before the whirring of helicopter blades filled the air. It must have been close by to get here so fast. She breathed a sigh of relief. Help was here, and Landon would no longer be able to ask her probing questions. When he looked at her with those dark brown eyes, she felt like he was looking right through her.

Landon watched as the search and rescue crew sent a man wearing climbing gear down the mountain. Because her injuries appeared to be minor, a litter was not required. Natasha was hooked into a harness and lifted onto solid ground. The helicopter landed so they could board. The pilot and the rest of the search and rescue team had already been given instructions to return him and Natasha to his vehicle and then do a search of the forest for Gary.

He wanted to go on the search himself, but his priority had to be with transporting Natasha to the hospital to make sure she didn't have any internal injuries. He'd be contacted if Gary was spotted. Russ, who was waiting back at the cabin in case Gary returned to his car, could catch the chopper to help with the search.

Where Gary had run was thick forest, no real trails or even a logging road for miles. Being a bush pilot meant that Gary had some survival training. But it would be dark soon. This time of year they had less than six hours of daylight. Landon's guess was that Gary would try to get back to civilization as quickly as possible.

The chopper gained altitude. And then angled off toward Natasha's cabin where he'd left his truck. Natasha sat beside him with a blanket wrapped around her.

"You doing okay?"

She nodded. She stared straight ahead. The bruises on her arm were starting to turn purple.

He totally hadn't bought her story about visiting family up north. Any time he'd come into the diner, she'd been friendly but only to a point. He really didn't know anything about her other than she'd showed up here over a year ago. When they touched down not too far from the cabin, Russ ran over to meet them.

"I arranged for Gary's stolen car to be towed. Mine

is locked up tight." Russ stared up at the sky. "We're losing daylight. We better find this guy."

Landon shouted above the whir of the helicopter blades. "My guess is he'll try to get back to a road as quickly as possible." He gave Russ a friendly slap on the back.

Russ boarded the helicopter. Landon wished they had more resources and manpower. If Gary didn't turn up before nightfall, he'd have to call Anchorage to see if he could get some help with a manhunt.

Natasha still held the blanket tight around her shoulders. She walked slowly, falling behind him.

He turned back to face her. "Let's drive you to the hospital. Get you checked out."

"I have to get my tires replaced for my trip."

"We can arrange for a tow to the garage." He stepped closer to her. "Look, you've been through a very traumatic day. Maybe you should think about postponing that trip."

She looked at him and then at the ground.

"I can't." She seemed agitated. "I have to get out of town." This time she met his gaze. Was that fear he saw in her eyes?

"We'll get you on the road as quickly as we can." Aware that shock might be settling in, he touched her lightly on the shoulder. "Come on, we need to make sure you didn't sustain any serious damage when you fell."

She nodded, giving a sideways glance to her cabin and defunct car. He opened the passenger door of his truck for her. She had buckled in by the time he sat behind the wheel. He turned, offering her a smile, hoping that would make her feel more comfortable.

She responded, though it was more of a spasm than a smile. He hadn't noticed before that her eyes were a greenish gray.

He turned the truck around and headed toward the main road. The hospital was on the outskirts of what passed for a town several miles up the road.

He drove for a few minutes, not sure what to say to her.

His phone rang. Russ's voice vibrated through the line. "No sign of him from the helicopter. I'm headed back to my vehicle to continue the search by patrolling the roads. I'll keep you advised."

"Ten-four. Are there any cabins in that area where he might have taken refuge or been able steal another car?"

"Not that we could see," Russ said.

"Keep looking," Landon said. "Once I transport Natasha, I'll go back on duty and see if we can't organize a little more manpower." He clicked his phone off.

"He's still out there, isn't he?" She sounded upset. She laced her fingers together.

"We'll catch him." He hoped he sounded reassuring.

"What if he tries to take Ezra again?" she asked.

"We're keeping a close watch on the boy and his mom and grandma." Deb, the trooper who had suffered minor injuries when Gary escaped, had volunteered for that duty. He didn't need to point out that Gary seemed to have turned his vengeful energy onto Natasha. She was agitated enough as it was.

"It's pretty awful for a little boy to have to go through that," she said.

That she showed concern for Ezra's safety more so than her own suggested that Natasha was capable of deep empathy, a quality his late wife had possessed.

"Can't argue with you there. The kid has been through a lot with the divorce being so contentious."

They drove on in silence for several minutes.

He checked his mirror, his brow furrowing. "We got miles and miles of road, and this guy has to be right on my bumper. He's been following us almost from the time we turned out onto the main road from your place."

Natasha turned her head. And then looked straight ahead, slamming her body against the back of the seat. "Slow down. See if he passes us."

"It's no big deal."

"Do what I say."

Landon's hackles went up a little. He was the driver. What was she doing ordering him around? But it was the terror in her voice that made him decide to slow down. It was clear she didn't trust him. Maybe humoring her would build a bridge.

The car zoomed around them.

The stiffness in her shoulders eased and she shook her head. "Sorry. I didn't mean to get snippy with you."

"No problem."

He focused on the road as it became curvier. He let up a little as they drove through a winding canyon. Once the road straightened out, he saw that the car that had passed them had gone off the road. It was pointed face-first toward a small drop-off. Why was the car not moving? It would have been easy enough to reverse and get back on the road.

"I've got to stop and make sure the driver is okay," Landon told her, pulling off to the side of the road. "He's not getting out of his car or pulling back onto the road. We might be dealing with someone who had a heart attack or something."

Most highway stops were routine, but he had to assume the worst-case scenario every time he checked on a driver. As his training dictated, he approached the vehicle on the passenger side of the car. The seat back was high enough that he couldn't see the driver's head. He stepped a little closer. The driver wasn't behind the wheel. Maybe he'd just stopped to go to the bathroom, but why go off the road in a way that made it look like there'd been an accident instead of just pulling over onto the shoulder? He caught a glimpse of a rifle in the backseat.

He had only half a second for alarm bells to go off before the sound of gunfire filled the air. He dove to the ground. The shots, which had come from a handgun, had been aimed at his vehicle, not at him. Landon couldn't get a good look at the shooter, who had likely shielded himself in the cluster of trees not far from the road. Clearly, they'd been set up.

His first thought was that Gary had somehow managed to steal a car and was coming after Natasha yet again.

Still on his stomach and turned around, Landon looked up toward the road. He saw that Natasha had gotten behind the wheel.

He crawled in the direction of the road as his truck rumbled toward him. Natasha drove in a serpentine pattern. Another shot was fired from the trees at his truck. When she got close to him, the passenger-side window went down and she shouted, "Get in."

He grabbed the door handle, opened the door and jumped in even as the vehicle rolled forward.

FIVE

Natasha's heart raced as she drove through the snow-covered grass that surrounded the road. She'd barely slowed down for Landon to jump into the passenger seat. He'd displayed a degree of athleticism in flinging open the door and jumping in while the vehicle was still moving.

She glanced in the rearview mirror. The man with the gun was running toward his car, preparing to give chase. Though she could not see his face clearly, his build made it clear it was not Gary.

"Do you mind telling me what is going on?"

"Later," she said. The cat was out of the bag. She'd have to tell him, just not right now. She pressed down on the accelerator and veered toward the road. "Let's try to shake this guy."

"You've done this before," Landon said.

They were headed back toward where they'd come from, toward wilderness and remote cabins. "Is there some back road or some other way into town?" she asked.

"Not that would be passable this time of year." He craned his neck. "He's right on your bumper."

"I see that," Natasha said. The needle eased past eighty. "I have the pedal pressed to the floor." High speed on the road this time of year was not a good idea. Patches of black ice were all too common.

The other vehicle slammed against her bumper. The impact was jarring. She bit her tongue. The hitman must have been waiting at the intersection where the road to her cabin met the main road. It hadn't taken the long arm of the mafia much time to figure out where she lived. The hitman must have come from close by. Plenty of people owed a debt to Leo Tan Creti.

Landon looked side to side. "There's a turnoff about a quarter mile up the road to the right. Wait until the last second to make the turn so he speeds past. He'll have to go a ways up the road before there's a spot for him to turn around. That should buy us time to get turned around and head in the other direction into town."

She nodded. Landon patrolled this road all the time. He probably knew every rock, tree and turnoff by heart.

"It's coming up here. It's a paved road just past that mile marker," he said.

"I see it." She kept her speed steady. Making the turn at such a high speed was going to be dicey. She passed the mile marker and let off the gas as she cranked the wheel. The turn was so tight, it felt as though the wheels on her side had lifted off the ground.

As predicted, the other car sped past.

They hit a patch of ice and spun. The truck veered toward an embankment then tipped and rolled. The seat belt pressed into her skin. They banged around and came to a stop upside down. She stared through the windshield, which had become a thousand tiny diamonds.

Landon was already clicking out of his seat belt. "We need to get out of here."

Still stunned, Natasha oriented herself to the upsidedown console in front of her.

"He's going to be coming for us, right? I'll call for help as soon as we can get to a safe place." He pushed the passenger-side door open. It made a screeching sound as it moved on the hinges, probably because it had been bent in the accident.

She fumbled for the release button on her seat belt. By the time she was out of it, Landon had come around to her side of the truck and yanked the door open. She twisted around so she could crawl out on her belly. When she stood, she had only a second to register that the hitman's car had turned off the main road and headed in their direction.

"We have to go where a car can't get to us," Landon said.

She glanced over his shoulder as fear gripped her heart.

The car was a hundred yards away and barreling toward them.

He tugged on her hand and pulled her away from the road. They sprinted for the forest, Natasha falling in behind Landon as he ran in a seemingly random pattern. The trees and undergrowth thickened.

A gunshot resounded through the air, glancing off a tree trunk not far from her head. Now the guy was using the rifle.

"Let me take up the rear," Landon said as he slowed his pace. "Whatever happens to me, don't slow down."

He'd shifted into position behind her to make him the more likely target. She'd be somewhat shielded. The move struck Natasha as very sacrificial. Maybe it was his sense of duty as a trooper that drove him.

Her leg muscles strained as she tried to run faster. Two more shots were fired, each close enough to cause a ringing in her ears. Her heart pounded and she struggled for breath. They kept running uphill through even more forest. The sky turned gray as the sun dipped low on the horizon. This time of year, the sun set by four o'clock.

In another hour, they would be traveling in total darkness. Their running slowed to a jog as both of them started to fatigue. It had been a good ten minutes since any shots had been fired or she'd heard any sound that indicated the hitman was close.

Slowing to a brisk walk, she spoke in a breathless whisper. "Do you think we lost him?"

Landon stopped and listened. He kept his voice soft, as well. "Not sure." He pulled his phone out. The screen illuminated his face. "I don't have a signal. Let's keep moving. I need to figure out where we are."

It grew darker. The temperature dropped at least ten degrees. Her winter coat kept her core warm, but she could feel the chill on her exposed skin.

They stepped around a fallen log. Landon stopped for a moment and stared at the sky. "Wish it wasn't so cloudy. Once it's totally dark, I'd be able to use the stars to figure out which way is north. I say we head in the general direction that should lead us back to the road."

"That makes sense. We'll just head downhill." Though it appeared that the hitman had given up, there was a danger they could run into him if they headed for the main road, especially if he'd returned to his car and was patrolling the road.

"The other troopers should find my wrecked truck," he said. "They'll know something is up."

She hoped that was true. Searching in the dark would be a challenge.

They headed back downhill. The trees grew sparser as the incline became steeper. Landon briefly used the flashlight app on his phone to figure out the best way down.

Natasha found herself testing each footstep before moving forward. Up ahead, she saw nothing but the shadows of trees. She looked over her shoulder. Light flashed in the distance.

Her heartbeat sped up. "He's still behind us."

"I saw it, too. Let's just keep moving. I won't turn my flashlight on again until I'm sure we've lost him."

They moved as quietly and quickly as possible. After they'd been walking for at least an hour, Landon stopped. "I know there's not much traffic after dark, but we should be hearing the sound of the road by now."

She turned and studied the landscape behind her, not seeing any light or movement. "We must be going the wrong way."

He didn't respond. Instead he shifted direction and kept walking.

"If they did find your wrecked truck, wouldn't they send the search and rescue chopper out again?"

"Seems like it," Landon said. "They're probably concentrating their efforts on trying to capture Gary."

"Is anybody expecting you anywhere tonight?"

"I didn't have any plans other than going home," he said. "What can I say? I'm just Mr. Excitement."

She laughed. "I'm kind of the same way." The joke provided some momentary levity in an otherwise bleak situation. Because she wanted to maintain a low profile, her life consisted mostly of working at the diner and staying at home.

They kept walking. She zipped her ski jacket tighter around her neck as it continued to grow colder.

Landon stopped abruptly on a flat area that looked like a wide trail. "I have an idea where we are." He switched on his phone's flashlight again, revealing a pile of rocks that someone had stacked to form a sort of triangle. "If I'm right, there's an off-the-grid cabin on the other side of these trees and down a hill. I know the owner. He only uses it seasonally. We can shelter there for few hours, get our energy back and warm up. Now that I know where we are, I might be able to get us back to the road."

He picked up his pace and Natasha followed him.

She said a prayer of thanks that Landon knew the area so well. They moved through the forest and down a rocky incline. The cabin was hidden by trees.

The door was pad-locked. "No worries," Landon assured her. "The owner asked me to check on it during the off season." He stepped off to the side of the cabin, lifted a rock and pulled out a small container. "He leaves me a key to make sure the mice haven't taken over inside."

He unlocked it and pushed the door open, gesturing that she should go first. In the darkness, she could make out only the outlines of furniture and some canned goods on a shelf. As Landon worked his way over to a corner of the room, she could hear him shuffling around.

"Can you hold the light so I can get this lantern lit?"

Natasha stepped toward him, taking the phone. The screen revealed that there was still no signal. She aimed the phone at his hands.

Light spread through the cabin. Now she could see all of it. It was maybe twelve feet by twelve feet. With a table and an area for sleeping. A basin and a camp woodstove stove rested on a counter area.

"Not exactly the Ritz, but I'm not complaining," she said.

Landon stepped over to the only window and drew the curtain. "We can't risk the light being seen."

She sat on the large wooden platform that must suffice for a bed. The owner probably didn't leave any bedding behind because it would be too tempting to the mice to turn it into their new home.

Landon paced the floor. "The guy comes up here in the warmer months to fly-fish. He hauls his water from the river. I know it's cold, but building a fire might draw the shooter to us."

She shrugged. "This will do. Like you said, we can hike out when we are rested and maybe have some light." Certainly, by then someone would be searching for Landon. Even if no one would miss her. Tomorrow was her day off, so she wasn't even expected at the diner.

"That seems like the smart thing to do. We'll only get more lost in the dark and cold." Landon sat in the only chair.

"Of course, sunrise isn't until almost ten."

"True. Let's just rest and get warmed up." He placed the lantern on the floor between them. "Now, how about you tell me why that man was shooting at you?"

Natasha's stomach tightened. She couldn't hide the truth from him any longer.

By the glow of the lantern, Landon studied the woman who had almost gotten both of them killed. "That guy chasing us… He's not out to get me, is he? He shot at my truck when you were behind the wheel."

Natasha looked off to the side and then shook her head. "No, it's me he wants dead." Her voice quivered.

Her auburn hair had come loose from the tight braid she kept it in. Wisps of hair surrounded her face. The flickering light danced on her skin. She didn't seem defensive. She seemed almost fearful.

"So, either you came up to Alaska 'cause you got into some kind of trouble down in the Lower 48—" she still wasn't looking him in the eyes "—or you are in witness protection."

Even if she was in hiding, Landon knew it didn't necessarily mean she was law-abiding. Plenty of people in WITSEC rolled on their fellow criminals and disappeared into a new life courtesy of the United States government. In all his brief interaction with her at the diner, though, nothing about Natasha suggested she had ever been on the wrong side of the law.

The fact that she had risked her life to ensure Ezra had been brought home safe spoke volumes about her character.

She drew her knees up to her chest and rocked back and forth. "Once that news story started to spread, I knew I needed to get out of here. For reasons of revenge—the mafia wants me dead."

He nodded. "I'm sorry that news crew showed up."

"You had no way of knowing. I have to leave Little

Bear. It's not safe for me. As soon as I can get in touch with the US Marshal I know I can trust…" She let out a heavy breath. "I'm going to have to be relocated again."

"Why don't you let me help you in the meantime?"

She looked at him. Even in the dim light, her gaze was piercing. "No one else can know."

"Your secret is safe with me."

"Please understand. Where I used to be, it didn't matter if someone wore a uniform. Some people can be bought, some are just trying to protect the ones they love."

Landon thought he saw tears rimming her eyes. "We'll figure this out when we get back to town. Why don't we try to sleep?"

"You have to comprehend what we are dealing with here. That hitman may have given up for the night or he might still be looking. But trust me, in the morning, he will have had time to call in reinforcements," she said. "He doesn't get paid until I'm dead. That's how it works." Placing her feet back on the floor, she rested her palm on her forehead and stared at the ceiling as though she were fighting off the need to cry.

Landon felt a tightness through his chest as a chill ran over his skin. Natasha had kept this secret for a year. He was sure that she spent a lot of time looking over her shoulder and feeling very alone in her fight. "I get it. We're dealing with some really dangerous people. We'll figure this out together." The gravity of what she had told him sunk in. "I think I'll keep watch for a while."

"I don't know if I can sleep."

He took off his coat and folded it. "Use this for a pillow. It might help."

"Won't you be cold?" she said.

"I've got layers upon layers on. This place is pretty well insulated."

After taking the coat, she tucked her legs up toward her chest and lay her head on the makeshift pillow. She flipped over once. A few minutes later her breathing indicated she'd fallen asleep.

Landon remained alert and listening for a least an hour before sleep overtook him. He awoke with a start to the sound of breaking glass.

SIX

Landon's panicked voice jerked Natasha from a deep sleep to fully alert.

"Get down, we're being shot at!" He pulled her to the floor. "Under here." He pointed at the storage area under the bed platform.

Her heart pounded as she rolled under the bed that would provide some shelter from the ricocheting bullets in the tiny cabin. She peered out as Landon pressed in close to her in the tiny space. Glass spread across the wood floor of the cabin. Three shots had been fired.

Silence fell around them. She could hear the sound of Landon's breathing as well as her own. Thirty seconds that felt like forever ticked by.

What was the hitman doing? Why had he stopped shooting? She whispered her next thought, knowing that the assassin might be right outside the window. "He didn't stop because he's out of bullets. He's a pro. I'm sure he brought extra clips with him."

Landon leaned close to her ear. "My thoughts exactly. I think he's waiting for us to come out so he can pick us off one at a time. Now that he's scared us, he's counting on us trying to run."

There were only two ways out of the cabin: through the door or the broken window. "He has a gun, though. What if he decides to enter the cabin?"

Landon seemed to be weighing options, as well. His gaze darted around the room. And then up to the ceiling. Make that three ways out of the cabin. He tugged on her sleeve and pointed up at a skylight. The hitman couldn't watch the window, the door and the skylight.

"I say we wait him out, so he becomes more anxious or loses focus and then we climb out." The game they were playing was a psychological one. This guy was a pro. He was used to having to wait for an opportunity to kill, but even a pro would grow impatient after a while. If they kept quiet, maybe he would wander away from the cabin or decide to check to see if they were even inside.

Landon nodded. "I'll take up a post by the door. In case he does decide to come in, I can hit him in the back of the head before he has a chance to shoot you." He pulled himself out from beneath the shelter of the tiny space and moved slowly across the floor on his stomach.

Natasha winced when a floorboard creaked where his boot scraped. Landon froze in place for a second.

She felt the sensation of having headphones on as her heartbeat thrummed in her ears. No sound came from outside the cabin. Satisfied, Landon crawled on all fours took up a position kneeling by the door. She allowed at least fifteen minutes to pass, keeping her ears tuned to any sound outside. All she heard was tree branches swaying in the breeze.

Crawling on her belly, Natasha dragged herself out from beneath the bed platform. Crouching, she pushed herself to her feet and stepped across the floor. When she stepped on broken window glass, her boot crunching the glass sounded like paper being crinkled. She took up a position beneath the broken window and slowly raised her head so just her eyes were above the windowsill. It was still dark. Her gaze darted around, seeing only the evergreens. No movement, no color suggesting that the hitman was on this side of the cabin, either close to it or on the other side of the trees. She turned toward Landon and shook her head.

They waited for another twenty minutes or so without hearing any noise. Her muscles grew stiff. Crouching she made her way back to the center of the room and scooted the cabin's only chair so it was beneath the skylight. When she looked over at Landon, he nodded. She got on the chair, careful not to make any noise.

She glanced across the room. If the hitman walked past the window, he would see her. She stretched her arms up and pushed the skylight open. Cold air swirled around her. It would take substantial effort to pull herself through the skylight.

Landon must have picked up on her hesitation. He made his way across the room and laced his hands together, making a stirrup for her to use. As he pushed her from beneath and she pulled up, gripping the rim of the skylight, she was keenly aware of the amount of noise they were making. It wasn't a racket, but any noise could alert the hitman if he was close by. She lifted the skylight only another inch so the motion wouldn't call attention to her or get her shot if the assassin was looking at the roof.

She looked toward the river. The sun still hadn't come up, but she could make out the outlines of her surroundings at least. The tree branches were thin enough this high up that she could see the area around the cabin. She spotted the hitman even though he wore clothes that made him blend into his surroundings. He was headed for the cabin, head down, gun in his hand. Maybe he'd gone to the river for a drink or to go to the bathroom. It didn't matter this was their chance for escape. They had only seconds to act before he'd be close to the cabin.

She dropped back down with a thud. "We can get out of here through the front door if we hurry."

Landon said nothing. Instead he turned and sprinted toward the door. She was right behind him. He swung the door open. The hitman would be close enough now to hear them. Both of them sprinted outside and through the trees that surrounded the cabin.

They ran through the darkness.

A shot rang out behind them. She didn't have to look over her shoulder to know that the hitman was right on their heels. Landon veered off toward the cover of some rocks and trees, but slipped on an icy patch, catching himself by putting a hand out to stop his fall. She followed, pumping her legs. Out of the corner of her eye, she saw movement as the assassin edged toward them. He was getting close enough to have a clean shot.

They hurried toward the trees. Landon seemed to know where he was going as he glanced around while still moving and then chose a path that led up a hill in a zigzag pattern. When the forest opened up, they headed downhill.

Off in the distance, she saw smoke rising above the trees. A cabin. As the sky changed from black to gray, she spotted more signs of civilization, various houses and barns dotting the landscape in the distance.

Finally, she heard the sound of cars rolling across pavement. They were close to the main road. Both of them slowed their pace. She turned slightly, not seeing any sign of the hitman.

"I think we lost him."

"Let's not count on that. He's been tenacious in hunting us down."

The assassin did seem to have some keen tracking skills to have found them at the cabin. Judging how quickly the hitman had gotten to Natasha's house in the first place meant that he must already have been close to Little Bear. She had not gotten a look at his face.

They came out onto the road. Landon tilted his head toward the sky. "I'm not sure why they aren't looking for us. Seems like we would have seen a chopper by now." He squeezed her shoulder. "Let's see if we can hitch a ride into town and get to the trooper station."

The last place Natasha wanted to be was in Little Bear. Even if they had managed to escape him this time, the assassin was still out there. She needed to stick with her original plan and escape to somewhere where she could fade into the background until she could contact Marshal Henderson. Waiting for her car to be fixed seemed foolhardy. There had to be another way out of town. A bus or something.

As they walked along the road, waiting for a car to come along, she scanned the hill they'd just run down. The hitman could still come after them. Traffic on this road was always light and, so far, they hadn't encountered any cars. She felt vulnerable out here in the open. Once again, she felt the urgency to get out of town. As long as she stayed in this area, she had a target on her back.

A car appeared, slowing as it eased past them.

Landon waved. "I know that guy. That's Melvin. He owns the hardware store in town."

They ran toward the idling car. The man rolled down his window. Resting his hand on top of the car, Landon leaned in.

"What's going on? You look like you've been fighting with a grizzly all night, Landon." Melvin glanced at Natasha as recognition spread across his face.

She thought he looked vaguely familiar. He must have come into the diner. He certainly wasn't a regular.

"It's a long story. We could use a ride into town."

"Hop in," Melvin said.

Landon offered Natasha the front passenger seat. "I can sit in back," she said. Melvin would probably expect small talk if she sat up front. She just didn't have the energy for that given what the last twenty-four hours had been like.

She clicked her seat belt in as Melvin pulled back out onto the road. As expected, Landon kept the conversation with Melvin going. Then Landon pulled out his phone, saying he needed to make some calls.

Natasha rested her back against the seat and closed her eyes. Landon's voice seemed to get farther away as she listened to him talk. His first call was to get his truck towed. The second sounded like he was talking to another trooper.

From the conversation, she gathered that Gary had been taken into custody. The manhunt had kept law enforcement busy. They had just gone by Landon's house and started to worry that something had happened to him.

Gary's capture was good news at least.

Her plan hadn't changed. She knew it was up to her to get out of town and to find a place to hide until WITSEC could help her escape into another identity and a new location.

Landon put away his phone as Melvin slowed when they reached the city limits of Little Bear. Main Street with its two stoplights was a welcome sight. Melvin pulled in behind the hardware store. It was too early for the store to be open, but Melvin lived in an apartment above the store.

"Thanks for the ride," Landon said.

Natasha opened her eyes and clicked out of her seat belt.

"You want to come with me down to the station?" he asked, turning to her.

She didn't answer right away. She glanced nervously toward Melvin. "I guess."

She was probably worried that Melvin would start to wonder why she'd been with him on the road and start asking questions. He hadn't intended to give away any part of her secret.

They both stepped out of the car. Melvin got out, as well, offering them a wave as he went into the back entrance of the hardware store.

They circled around the building to Main Street. Natasha hesitated on the street corner.

"If it's all the same to you," she said, "I think the best thing for me to do is to figure this out on my own. The longer I stay in Little Bear, the more dangerous it becomes. I appreciate all that you have done, but I don't want you to be hurt at my expense."

"Natasha, maybe I can help you."

"I think it would be better if I got out of town alone." She walked ahead of him.

He hurried to catch up with her. "Look, I'm law enforcement around here. Maybe I can make some calls."

"No. I don't want to get a bunch of people involved." She walked even faster until she stepped on the curb. She crossed her arms over her chest and turned to face him. "I can't risk the information about my new placement being leaked out even if your contacts are trustworthy. What if the wrong eyes see where I'm being moved? It happened once before. Alaska wasn't my first placement. I can't take the chance." She turned and started walking.

"Where are you going to go?"

"A bus comes through here, doesn't it?"

"Twice a week."

"Maybe I can buy a car off of somebody," she said. "I have some money saved."

He wasn't sure why, but it hurt his feelings that she wanted to leave him. "Come down to the station until we can sort things out."

She stopped, shoving her hands into her coat pockets. "What's to be sorted out? I need a hiding place." She turned and kept walking.

"Okay, I'll help you find a hiding place. I want you to be safe. It's in my job description to take care of the citizens of Little Bear."

She slowed a little in her pace.

"I have to go down to the station to borrow a trooper vehicle until I can get my truck towed. I'm not sure if it will even run. I can at least give you a ride somewhere. Everyone will see you walking through the town. If that guy comes and starts asking questions, he'll be able to track you down."

Natasha turned to study him, pressing her lips together and looking to the side as if weighing her options. "I'll wait outside the station."

"You do what you think you need to do. I don't think any of the other troopers will be around anyway. One of them is transporting Gary, and the other is probably home sleeping. I'll take you out to my house. Maybe you will be able to get in touch with your guy and we can get the ball rolling on getting you to a safe house while they try to set you up somewhere."

She looked at him for a long moment while they stood on the sidewalk. Because sunrise was so late this time of year, the town woke up slowly. It would still be a couple hours before sunrise. A car that looked a lot like the hitman's rolled by slowly.

Natasha's body jerked and she pressed a little closer to Landon. He saw the fear in her eyes.

Landon waved at the driver. "It's okay. I know him."

"You said yourself the hitman might be a local."

Landon said, "We have no way of knowing. I never saw his face. I do know there are a lot of cabins around here. Alaska is a good place for someone with ties to the mafia to hide. This guy might have been retired but owed someone some favors."

Once again, Landon hurried to catch up with her. He wished that there was something he could do or say to ease her fear.

"We can't stay in that trooper vehicle for too long. It's too recognizable. It makes me an easy target. The hardware store guy knows I'm with you. It's just a matter of time." She spoke in a rapid-fire manner and looking straight ahead. Her feet tapped out a rhythm that matched the intensity of her words, in a hurry with intention.

It seemed to be getting colder. When he tilted his head at the overcast sky, it looked like a storm was on the way.

"I have another vehicle at my house. I have a snow-mobile. We can get away on cross-country skis." He intended the remark about the skis to be a joke, anything to lighten the tension. More than anything, he wished that she'd trust him more.

Natasha stopped abruptly. "Please don't treat this like a joke."

Mentally he kicked himself. "I'm sorry. I was just trying to lighten things up. I don't want you to be so afraid. I'm here to help you."

The look on her face devastated him. It was as if a shadow had fallen over her features. He saw in her eyes that she didn't believe him.

"I just need to get to someplace safe where that hit-man can't find me." Her voice was a monotone as she talked, but her eyes were glazed with tears.

He turned and stared up the street. They were less than a block from the station. He couldn't begin to understand what she had been through. For the past year, she'd had only herself to rely on. He nodded. "Let's go get that trooper vehicle. I'll just give you my car. When you're able to get set up, communicate through the marshal where you left the car and I'll make arrangements to get it back."

Though he had tried to hide it, she must have picked

up on the hurt he was feeling at her rejection of his offer to help. Her voice softened. "That is a really generous offer. Thank you."

They arrived at the station house. She waited outside, tucked under the shadow of the eaves, while he went in to get the keys for the only remaining trooper vehicle. As he had assumed, none of the other troopers were present. Angie, the dispatcher, was in a room at the far end of the building on the other side of the two jail cells.

When he returned outside, he found Natasha waiting on the back end of the building that faced the parking lot by thealley where the vehicles were kept She had tucked in close to the building, probably so that if someone did go down the alley, they wouldn't notice her.

Snow had started to swirl out of the sky.

It tugged at his heart to see her there. So vulnerable and so alone in the world, and so afraid to accept his offer of help. As a lawman, he felt a sense of duty toward her. Maybe she thought she could only rely on herself, but he wasn't comfortable with just sending her out into the dangerous world that was now her life.

He stepped up to her and waved the keys. "Let's get moving. I live about four miles outside of town."

She nodded glanced side to side as she stepped away from the building. Once they were both buckled in, Landon rolled through the alley and pulled out onto the street. They'd reached the outskirts of town when he checked his rearview mirror and saw a newer model truck behind him that he didn't recognize as belonging to one of the locals.

Not unusual, tourists came through here all the time.

And the hitman had been driving a car. Still, he knew that, from now on, he had to assume that the threat on Natasha's life could come back at them at any moment.

SEVEN

As they left the city limits, Natasha could feel her anxiety rising. The snowfall had intensified and the wind was blowing it sideways. The wipers on the SUV worked frantically to keep the window clear. The impending bad weather only added to the fear she was already wrestling with. At least, she should have been on her way out of town by now.

How long would it be before the hitman came after her again? The hardware store owner knew she was with Landon. Another person had seen them together on the street. As kind as Landon seemed, she knew she couldn't stay long at his house. The offer of the car was very generous.

Too, she felt guilty that he had become a target simply by being with her. Landon seemed like a man who had a strong sense of duty, but there was no reason for his life to be in danger, too.

She put her hand in her pocket, where the tiny wooden nativity still was. God was with her. She could figure this out by herself.

Landon sped up. He drove for about ten minutes, passing several houses that were far apart, most having barns or airplane hangars.

"What if your truck isn't in good enough shape to drive when it gets towed?"

"Then I can't loan you the car," he said. "We'll come up with another plan. You can try getting hold of your marshal again. Maybe he has some ideas." His voice held a note of compassion.

"If I can't borrow your car, I'll figure out something," she said.

"How many times do I have to say it? I want to make sure you're safe. That's my job. I'm not just kicking you to the curb."

He seemed almost irritated with her.

"I'm sorry you got dragged into this. I never meant for that to happen," she said.

Before he could answer, he had to turn his attention to the road as the SUV slid on a patch of black ice. Landon gripped the steering wheel and maneuvered the SUV back into the proper lane just as another vehicle appeared around a curve in the opposite lane.

Visibility had been reduced to only a few feet.

"This storm sure came on fast and hard," he said.

She turned her head and checked behind her. She could just make out the blurry glow of another set of headlights. She couldn't see what kind of car it was.

He turned down a long driveway. Once they were close enough, a small house came into view as they rounded a curve. A shop that had garage doors and a people-size door stood beside the house. The wrecked truck stood in the driveway. His car must be in the shop.

He peered through the windshield. "I don't think anybody is going anywhere until this storm lets up."

Her spirit deflated. He was right, of course. But that

didn't do anything to dampen the sense of urgency she felt as they both got out of the SUV. The wind caused the snow to feel like a thousand tiny swords stabbing at her exposed skin.

No lights were on in the house. He placed a hand on the middle of her back. "Come on, let's get inside before we freeze."

Natasha took a quick backward glance down the road they had just driven. She couldn't see more than ten feet or so. Even if that car behind them had been the hitman's, he wouldn't be so obvious as to follow them down a private road right away.

Landon dug the keys out of his pocket and ushered her into his house. She stepped into an open area that had a small kitchen and living room. An overstuffed chair with a pile of books beside it stood close to the woodstove. There was a couch pushed off in a corner. The stack of folded clothes that covered it suggested it wasn't used for sitting anymore.

Landon hurried into the living room. "Let me get the fire going and warm it up in here. It's been hours since I was home."

He disappeared through a back door and returned a moment later holding several pieces of wood.

"I can help you haul the logs." She hurried across the room.

"That would be great," he said, leading her to the back door.

She stepped out the door onto a porch where the wood was stacked. Despite the protection of the porch, the wind seemed to be howling around her. She scanned the trees close enough to see through the driving snow. Her heartbeat kicked up a notch. The hitman would be hindered by the storm, too, but that didn't mean he wouldn't try to get at her.

"Are there any other roads that lead into your property?" she asked.

"Yes. There's a road that goes by the back of my house." Landon placed a log in the crook of his elbow. He followed the line of her gaze. "You know, maybe it would be best if you went back inside and stayed there for now."

"You're probably right." She hurried inside and sat in the easy chair. Landon was right about the storm. It would be foolish to try to drive anywhere until it let up, but staying here made her feel like a sitting duck.

Landon came inside and put kindling into the woodstove. Once it caught fire, he stacked the smaller logs in a teepee around the rising flames. Within minutes, the fire was crackling. Landon closed the door on the woodstove. "It'll warm up in no time."

Feeling numb from her inability to do anything, Natasha managed a nod. He rose from where he'd been crouching to give her shoulder a squeeze that was probably meant to be supportive as he walked past the chair.

Heat started to come off the stove and circulate in the room while she watched the flames dance.

Landon had stepped across the room and opened a drawer. He pulled his gun out of a utility belt and put the clip in the bottom. He was preparing for the worst, too.

She rose. "Do you have a personal gun I could use?"

He sat his semiautomatic down on the table closest to the door. "Look, I know you're scared, but a lot of times, giving a gun to someone without experience is a bad idea."

"I know how to handle a weapon. I used to be a police officer."

He didn't answer right away. She was sure a mil-
lion questions were raging through his head. Finally,
he nodded. "Okay."

He disappeared down a hallway. She was grateful
he hadn't asked any more questions. Though she was
sure the longer she stayed with him, the more he would
want to know.

The photos on the wall caught her attention. There
were pictures of Landon posing by a kayak and another of him holding the fish he'd caught. Several of
the images featured him with people who were probably siblings or cousins, judging from the resemblance.
Another photo, where Landon looked maybe ten years
younger, showed him on cross-country skis with a dog
beside him. There were three photos of him with a
blond woman at restaurants, outside this house and beside a trailhead sign. The woman's soft smile seemed
to radiate hope and love. That must have been his wife.

Landon returned, holding a gun. She looked away
from the photo of Landon with his wife, feeling like she
had peered in on something very private. She needed
to be very tight-lipped about her life and yet his was
on full display.

He handed her the Glock and two magazines. "I
have an extra clip for it. Already loaded."

She jammed the magazine into the pistol and set it
beside his gun. The other loaded magazine she put in
her pocket. "Thank you for trusting me about the gun."
The weight of the loaded magazine reminded her that
she was not safe yet.

He nodded. His gaze rested on her long enough for

her to feel uncomfortable. She took a step back, glancing at the wall of photos and then at him. She wanted to know more about his wife and his family, even what had happened to the dog in the photo. She wasn't sure what to ask that didn't sound like prying.

"Those photographs are just gathering dust. They were all taken a lifetime ago. I should remove them from the wall." A note of sadness seemed to permeate his voice.

Her own heart squeezed tight. The longing to share who she was and what she had been through was almost overwhelming. She understood the chasm of the loss he'd experienced. "I think you should dust them off and keep them on the wall. It's the story of your life, right?" She hoped her words offered some level of comfort.

"It's the story of the life I used to have." Landon turned toward the kitchen. "You must be hungry. Can I fix you something to eat?"

It was clear he didn't want to talk anymore about the past. As if on cue, her stomach growled. "I'm starving actually. That sounds great." She hadn't eaten since she'd been on her shift at the diner.

He opened the refrigerator and then the cupboards. He stopped and gripped the countertop. His expression hardened as he pressed his lips together and shook his head. "You know, you're the first person besides my siblings to come into this house since Maggie died."

She stepped toward him. He turned his head and looked at her. "A loss like that changes everything," Natasha said. The expression softened as the anguish in his features seemed to melt away. This time, his gaze was less probing. She saw warmth in his eyes.

"Guess you understand what it's like to have your life pulled out from under you. You don't even get to keep photos of who you used to be."

She nodded, feeling an intense connection to him.

He threw up his hands, breaking the power of the moment between them. "Enough of this gloominess." There was a look of mischief in his eyes. "Have you ever had a fried bologna sandwich?"

"Can't say that I have."

"Well then, you are in for a treat."

"Can I borrow your phone? I'm going to try to get hold of the marshal."

He walked over to where he'd hung his coat across a chair and got it for her. When she dialed the memorized number, it didn't even ring. Maybe the phone was dead. Maybe the other marshal had left for the holidays. Maybe the storm was affecting service.

"Nothing?" Landon asked.

She shook her head.

Natasha watched as Landon pulled bread out of the cupboard and bologna and cheese from the refrigerator. As he set the cast-iron pan on the stove, she found herself wishing that she had taken the time to get to know him better in the year that Little Bear had been her home. He was a man with character and pain that ran deep.

Once the storm let up, she would never see him again.

After clicking on the burner, Landon poured a little oil in the cast-iron pan. "My brother and sister and I used to make these all the time."

Natasha entered the kitchen and leaned against the counter, watching him. "Very gourmet."

"When you live out in the middle of Nowhere, Alaska, and getting food supplies is a once-a-month event, bologna is one of the protein-rich foods that keeps for a long time." The grease in the pan began to sputter. He lifted the pan and angled it side to side. "You want to throw some bread in the toaster?"

"Sure." She turned, scanning the counter for the toaster, and then stepped sideways to grab the loaf of bread. She popped two slices in the toaster. He separated the bologna, which sizzled when he tossed the slices into the pan.

The interaction had a ring of familiarity to it that made his heart ache all over again. He and Maggie had spent endless hours in the kitchen cooking much more elaborate meals than fried bologna sandwiches. He hadn't counted on the rush of grief just having another woman in his house would cause after two years.

He separated the cheese slices while Natasha placed two more pieces of bread in the toaster and brought him the first two. He pulled down plates and laid the bread open on one of them.

Natasha paced through the kitchen, checking the front window. She was still nervous about the hitman coming at her again. The blizzard was in full force, making it hard to see anything but gusting snow being blown around.

"He has to contend with the storm just like we do, Natasha," Landon said as he pulled the bologna out of the pan and placed it on a napkin to absorb the grease. "We don't know if he's even out there."

"I know." She stepped away from the window but

continued her patrol through the house, checking the window in the living room, as well.

He assembled the sandwiches and brought the plates over to her. "Tell you what. Why don't we eat and then I'll do a perimeter check?" He knew he wouldn't be able to go far from the house. Too much risk of disorientation because of the reduced visibility. He'd been on calls where he'd a found frozen body only feet from the doorstep.

She found a seat by the woodstove and sat. "You don't have to do that. I don't want you to turn into a Popsicle just to make me feel safer." She took a bite of her sandwich. "Maybe that car wasn't even him following us. Could have been anyone, right?"

He nodded wishing that he could make her feel less on edge. "How's your sandwich?"

She took a bite. "It's really good."

The lights flickered. Natasha rose, still holding the sandwich, but the plate it had been on fell off her lap and onto the floor.

The room went black.

Her frightened voice seemed to echo in the dark. "What's going on?"

"Natasha, just stay where you are. The storm probably just took out the electricity. It happens." Landon put his hand out in front of him as he made his way toward the kitchen where he kept his flashlight. His fingers found the wall.

An unspoken thought hung between them. Maybe it wasn't the storm that had caused the electricity to go out.

He reached out, finding the counter. "Are you doing okay?"

"Yes," Natasha said.

He felt along the counter and then let his fingers run over the drawers. The first one he opened wasn't the one with the flashlight. His fingers touched the cold metal of silverware. The dark was disorienting. He felt along the side of the cupboards until his finger found another drawer handle. He slid it open, brushing over its contents until he found the flashlight.

In the living room, something crashed against something else. Natasha was moving around.

"What are you doing?"

"Getting away from the window. I thought I saw lights flash outside." She was still moving around. From the sound of it, rather clumsily.

"Are you sure?" Landon pressed the button on the flashlight, which created a bubble of illumination around him. He could see about five feet in front of him, with the rest of the room growing gradually dimmer.

He turned and aimed the flashlight toward the living room as he walked. Natasha was crouching behind a chair.

She shielded her eyes from the light when he aimed it at her. "I'm not sure about what I saw. There was a sort of quick orange glow. I know I'm jumpy. I could be wrong, but I think someone is outside."

He hurried over to her. "There is a road not too far from the back of my house through the trees. It could be the reflection of headlights of someone driving."

"Out in this weather?"

"Some people have no choice. Could be a snow-plow."

He reached her and knelt beside her. Before he even

touched her shoulder, he could sense her fear. "Come with me. The first thing we will do is check the breaker box. Let's stay together. We don't know anything yet."

He stood, glancing out the window but seeing only darkness and blowing snow. "Stay close to me. Let's go over and get the guns."

She stood, as well, and followed him. They both picked up their respective handguns.

"You doing okay?"

She nodded. "It's the dark that makes me so afraid. Sorry I lost it there."

"No problem. The breaker box is just down the hall. Follow me."

They moved slowly down the hallway, past the first bedroom that had served as Maggie's craft/painting room. He shone the light toward the window in the bedroom, checking to see what might be outside. He was suddenly aware of how much dust covered everything in the room. Funny how having another person in the house made him realize how it was more like a tomb that he hid in, almost as if he was pretending that Maggie was coming back.

"My wife spent a great deal of time here. I should clean it out."

"You do that sort of thing when you feel ready."

Her response was so filled with compassion, he wondered if she had lost someone important in her life. "It's been two years." He turned his attention along the hallway. "The breaker box is just down here."

Once they were at the end of the hallway, he flipped open the breaker box and shone the light on it. None of the breakers was blown.

"It could be something outside the house. A power

line that broke beneath the weight of the snow and wind," he said, though he suspected that that was not Natasha's theory about why they were in the dark.

She didn't say anything.

"We don't have a lot of choices here, Natasha. The woodstove will keep us warm and I've got a seventy-two-hour emergency kit, plus plenty of canned goods."

"I just wish I could have gotten out of town when I had the chance."

His guess was that she didn't like feeling this powerless. "Let's get settled in the living room where it's warm. I got sleeping bags and blankets. We'll take shifts keeping watch. Maybe this storm will break by sunrise."

She nodded and followed him back to the living room. He found another flashlight for her to use and then brought in sleeping bags and blankets. "I'll sleep on the floor. You can have the couch."

She settled on the couch and drew a blanket around her shoulders. "But we're taking shifts staying awake, right?"

What could he do to make her feel safer?

If the hitman had disconnected the electricity, if he was out there, for sure he wouldn't stay outside in the elements. Either he would seek shelter in his car, which wouldn't guarantee survival, or he would try to get into the house…or the shop. The guy had come here to kill Natasha. Sooner or later, he'd make his move.

He rose. "Look, I said I would do a perimeter check. We need to be proactive about this. If he is out there, maybe we can catch him." He retrieved some parachute cord from the seventy-two-hour kit that he kept in a lower kitchen cupboard.

She got up from the couch. "What are you doing with that?"

"Using it to find my way back to the house in case I get disoriented." He reached for his winter coat.

"I'll get suited up, too. I can stand on your porch with the flashlight to help you find your way back."

"Sounds good. You can hold one end of the cord. If I tug on it, that means I'm disoriented and I need you to pull me in." It looked like he had roughly ten yards of cording, which meant he have to come in and go through the back door to check the back of the house where Natasha thought she'd seen lights, but he could make it to the shop and back.

They both got suited up. He placed his handgun in his shoulder holster. Natasha, as well, placed her gun in her waistband. He found her a pair of gloves which she put on.

They stepped outside into the whirling snow. Visibility was close to zero. He handed her one end of the parachute cord. "Tie it around the post, but hold on to it, too. If I tug twice, it means he's not in the shop and I need you to pull me back in."

She gazed up at him. "Be careful."

He nodded and stepped off the porch. The snow stabbed his exposed skin. He pulled his balaclava up to his nose. Though he could not see the shop, he had momentary views of the ground. Keeping his head down, he walked slowly.

When he figured he should be close, he looked up. His breath was hot beneath the fabric covering his face. The wind gusted and he had a view of the shop for just a moment. The sun must be up by now, it was the storm that made everything so dark. With the cording wrapped around his wrist, he stepped with more confidence, reaching the door to his shop. Aware that he might be bracing for a fight, he placed the flashlight in his pocket and then pressed his body against the wall and pulled his weapon. With his free hand, he reached out for the doorknob and eased the door open.

Landon slipped inside the shop, his gun raised. The only noise was the shrill gusting of the storm outside. Leaving the door slightly ajar, he retrieved the flashlight and aimed it into the corners of his shop. He checked around the snowmobile and inside the car he had intended to loan Natasha.

Satisfied that no one was hiding in the shop, he moved back toward the slightly ajar door. The line of cording that would help him get back to the house went slack.

His heart squeezed tight as he gave it a tug. There was no response on the other end of the line. He pulled several feet of cord toward his chest and a rising sense of panic invaded his mind. The cord had been cut from the post. He tugged one more time.

His breath caught when there was still no response. Natasha had let go of the line. Something had happened to her.

Without the cording, he wasn't sure if he'd be able to make it back to the house without becoming disoriented and freezing to death.

EIGHT

While Natasha waited on the porch, holding the parachute cord, a gloved hand smashed against her mouth. She twisted, trying to break free. Her hands reached up to try to pry the hand off her mouth. In her struggle, she dropped the cording, Landon's lifeline to find his way back to the house. The flashlight, as well, fell from her fingers. She heard it hit the wooden planks of the porch floor and roll.

She reached to pull the gun out of her waistband. The thickness of her gloves made it hard to grasp. Her hand wrapped around the butt of the gun and she yanked it out. It would be impossible to get her finger inside the trigger guard with the gloves on.

Her assailant had readjusted his grip on her, so his arm held her neck in a lock. She opted to use the gun as a blunt weapon rather than what it was designed for. She pounded his forearm once, but the thickness of his winter clothing rendered her attack ineffective.

The man grabbed the wrist that held the gun and smashed it against something hard. Pain reverberated up her arm as she let go of the weapon.

Natasha's instinctual response was to try to get

away, but running into the storm would be suicide. She turned, reaching out to find the door that led inside the house. The man grabbed her again. She angled and twisted her body, kicking her assailant in the legs as he lifted her off the wooden planks of the porch floor.

Her head banged against a porch post, sending pain across her face and down the nerves in her neck. The blow caused her to stop struggling for just a moment, which allowed the man to get her into a hold, one arm wrapped around her waist and the other putting pressure on her neck from the back. She could see nothing but the whiteness of the blinding snow. The man seemed to be dragging her toward the house though he was probably as disoriented as she was.

She lifted her legs so that she would be heavier and harder to carry. The man grunted and let go of her, forcing her to put her feet down or fall. He grabbed her by the hood of her coat and dragged her back. She lifted her hand to her neck where her coat choked her. When she turned her head sideways trying to ease the strain on her neck, she caught a glimpse of the flashlight glowing where it had fallen on the porch.

She couldn't see the piece of cord at all. Landon might be stranded in the shop. Would he dare try to get back to the house?

The man held on to her while he banged around and fumbled. He must be trying to find the door. The overhang of the porch provided a degree of shelter from the storm, but there was no porch or interior lights.

She heard the door swing open and bang against the wall. He yanked on her coat hood, dragging her across the threshold and then let go of her.

Wind and cold faded as she found herself inside the

dark house. Before she could get a breath, blunt force pushed on her chest, causing her to stumble backward. She hit the edge of the kitchen counter with such force that pain shot up her spine. Her eyes searched but she could detect no movement, only the sense the attacker was close.

The outside door slammed shut. Now it seemed even darker, as if that were possible. Her assailant must have pushed her inside with such force to prevent her from trying to escape through the open door.

The only advantage she had was that she knew the layout of the house better than him. She felt for the edge of the counter with her gloved hand. The blackness was so enveloping that she could not even see her hand let alone the man who intended to kill her. His footsteps pounded toward her. She dropped to the floor and crawled on all fours through the kitchen and down the hallway where she and Landon had checked the breaker box.

She heard the man fumbling behind her and then a flashlight came on just as she reached the end of the hallway. She remembered an open door by the breaker box that had a stairway and crawled toward it. Once she was on the stairway, she closed the door at the bottom of the stairs, praying that it would lock. She pushed in the knob, and it froze in place.

Before she could even make it up the stairs, the man was wiggling the knob. By the time she made it to the top, he was banging his body against the door. He must not have a handgun or he would have used it by now. Maybe he'd lost it in the struggle, like she had hers.

Natasha could make out only shadows and silhouettes of objects. She pulled off her other glove and stashed it in her pocket. When she felt around, her hand brushed over textured fabric, an old love seat. The banging continued downstairs. Was there another way out of this room?

She ran her hand over several other objects, a workout bench and weights. She found the wall and felt along it, hoping to find a second door that she could exit through.

She found a window, which probably meant she would be crouching on the overhang of the porch or falling to the ground, back into the storm. Not an option.

The tone of the banging had changed. He must have found an object to use as a battering ram. Judging from the sound, he was in the process of splintering the door. She gathered up all the hand weights she could and moved to the top of the stairway.

When the man finally broke through the door, her eyes had begun to adjust to the darkness. He was a moving shadow, at least. She picked up the first weight and fired it down the stairs.

The groan told her she had hit her target. In rapid-fire succession, she tossed the weights down the stairs until she was out of them. The noises told her that some of them had hit her target and others had rolled down the stairs.

The house grew eerily silent.

The sound of her own breathing seemed to intensify.

Had she knocked the man unconscious, or was he waiting for her at the bottom of the stairs? Waiting for her to make a noise so he could pinpoint her location.

The seconds ticked by as she tuned her ears to every

sound. The old house creaked as the wind buffeted against the windows.

When she peered down the stairs, she saw only blackness. Her heart pounded as she remained frozen.

She heard a different kind of noise. A footstep perhaps. And then more creaking. He was coming up the stairs to get her. She whirled around and grabbed for where she thought the weight bench was. Her hands found the object she sought. She dragged the bench toward the top of the stairway and gave it a hefty shove.

Her assailant stumbled and groaned. He must be trying to climb over the bench on the narrow stairway. She patted her hands across the floor, finding the exercise bike, which she also shoved down the stairs.

Down below, the man struggled and swore. Finally, she pushed the love seat so it blocked the top of the stairs. Scraping and bumping noises told her that he was moving the exercise bike out of the way.

The tactics had only bought her a little time. While the man struggled to reach her, she moved across the floor on all fours, reaching out for the wall with the window.

She had no other options. Eventually, he would get up the stairs. She flung open the window. Snow, wind and cold assaulted her. She felt below the window. There was an overhang that she could crawl out upon. She knew she could not stay outside for long and, if she dropped from the overhang, the disorientation might make it hard for her to find the porch and the door back into the house.

She crawled through the window and worked her way to the edge of the overhang. The sun was probably up by now, but she saw nothing but whiteness.

Only the howling wind greeted her ears as it chilled her exposed skin on her face and hands. She'd taken her gloves off to pick up the weights. She fumbled for her glove but dropped it. The wind was so intense, it blew it away before she could pick it up. She managed to get the other glove on.

Her plan had so many holes in it. Could she drop from the roof without injury? Staying outside in the elements for too long meant she risked freezing to death. Even if she did manage to get back into the house and find a hiding place, the assailant would be hunting for her eventually.

Her exposed hand was already starting to feel numb as she worked her way across the overhang. She reached the edge and crawled over, hanging on to the edge of the porch roof. She let go and dropped to the ground.

Though the shop provided a degree of shelter, Landon knew it was not an option to stay there. Natasha would not have let go of the parachute cord unless she had been attacked. If she was in danger, he needed to get to her before it was too late.

The rope might still be useful to direct him toward the house if it hadn't been blown around too much. He picked up his end and moved toward the shop door. A gust of wind made him take a step back when he opened the door. His gaze traveled from the cord in his hand to where he could see it on the ground. His view of the orange cording was consumed by the storm within a few feet. He stepped through the door, closing it behind him. The wind and snow whirled around him as he stared at the ground.

He feared that he might be walking toward his demise. Though he was dressed for winter, if he got off track away from the house, the exposure to the freezing temperatures could lead to hypothermia, compromised mental faculties and, ultimately, freezing to death.

He stared down at the orange rope by his boot. The wind intensified, picking up the cording and moving it several feet. He shook his head. How many times had that already happened? He needed a better plan to get to the house.

He turned and headed back toward the garage. He was still close enough that each time the wind died down a little he could see the blue siding. He pushed forward. The wind acted almost like a solid object that he had to move through as he bent and took another step.

He reached out for the garage door and stepped inside. He'd already come up with a more viable plan. The large shop door that he opened to get the car and snowmobile in and out was not electric, which meant he could push it open by hand. It had been hung on a pulley system that could be moved manually. He pushed the door open, feeling the biting intensity of the wind and snow all over again.

Then he climbed into the car he had intended to loan Natasha, started it up and switched on the headlights. He pulled out of the shop and turned the steering wheel in the general direction he thought was the house. There were ten yards of separation between the shop and the house. The view through his windshield was nothing but a solid sheet of white with momentary pockets of clearing that revealed only vague outlines.

Maybe Natasha had become disoriented and let go of the cording. That would be the best-case scenario, though it didn't seem possible. She had been standing beneath the shelter of the porch and would have been able to take the four or five steps to find the door easily enough.

Landon clenched his teeth. He knew the most likely scenario was that she'd been right about the assassin following them and that she'd been attacked.

He prayed she had managed to stay alive. He knew that he had wasted precious minutes trying to figure out how to get back to the house. His boot pressed the gas with a featherlight touch and he eased the car forward, hoping, praying, that something would come into view.

The tires rolled over the snow. Still, he could see nothing. His bumper hit something solid. He let up on the gas for a moment, listening to the engine hum. He tried to remember what object lay between his house and shop. A wheelbarrow or old tire, or maybe he'd hit the edge of the porch. Only one way to find out. He eased the car forward again. Whatever the object was, his car bumper could move it.

Feeling a rising sense of urgency, he backed up and turned the wheel, hoping to drive around the object. Again, he pressed the gas.

He jerked at the sound of someone or something banging on the hood of his car. The noise grew louder and then stopped. Then a different sound reached his ears. Someone was fumbling for the passenger door handle.

The door swung open. A blast of cold hit him and then a face came into view. Natasha's face, though it was red from exposure to the cold. Snow had frozen to her hood, which she had drawn over her head.

Her voice was almost a whisper. She clearly had been out in the cold for some time. "I saw the head-lights."

"Get in."

She stared at him for a long moment as though she was trying to process what he had said.

He patted the passenger seat. "Natasha, get in the car."

This time she complied. He saw then that one of her hands no longer had a glove. It, too, had turned red from exposure. He grabbed it and held it between his own two hands.

She was shivering.

He let the car idle and turned up the heat.

"Switch off the headlights. He might be able to see them."

"He's in the house?"

She nodded as she closed her eyes.

As he held her icicle of a hand between his, he knew this was no time to pump her for information. First, she needed to warm up.

He let go of her hand and grabbed one of his gloves where he'd left it on the console so he could drive. "Give me your hand." He could not see in the dim light if her fingertips were blue, which would mean frostbite had set in. "Are your fingers numb?"

She lifted her hand so he could put the glove on it. "It was only a few minutes that I was outside. I had to crawl out on the roof. I fell in the snow when I dropped down." She closed her eyes again, as though reliving what had happened was too much to face. "I rolled away from the house, and I couldn't find it."

He turned to check the backseat to see if he had

anything that might be of use. He spotted an old dog blanket, which he reached around and grabbed. "I hope you don't mind. This is covered in fur."

"If it will help warm me up, I don't care."

He placed the blanket over her torso.

She looked straight ahead as she drew the blanket up toward her chin. "Another couple of minutes and I could have frozen to death. I could feel my mind going numb, unable to make good choices."

He touched her shoulder. "But you didn't. You found me."

"God has always taken care of me through everything."

The level of faith she displayed in such trying circumstances made Landon realize that his own faith had in many ways sat dormant since Maggie's death. He'd gone to church, read his Bible and gone through the motions of praying. But really, there was part of him that had closed his heart off to God. "That's an amazing thing to say. Considering all that you have lost and all that you have been through."

"God is the one constant in my life."

He nodded. He wished that he could believe that. He turned and stared through the windshield, which provided a view of nothing but driving snow. The truth was that he didn't trust God anymore. Warmth and the hum of the car heater surrounded him. "Do you suppose he's still in that house?"

She pulled the blanket even closer to her neck and shuddered. "If he's smart, he'll stay in there. He's got to figure that we won't stay out here."

"At the first break in the storm, he'll try to come at you again if he realizes that you're still alive."

"These guys are thorough. I'm sure he has to produce a picture of me dead before he gets paid."

"Maybe…" Landon suggested, "we can get back into the house and take him out. Arrest him before the storm breaks."

Her response did not come right away as the options and the possibilities tumbled through her head. "Even if we put him in jail, Leo Tan Creti will just send someone else." She let out a heavy breath.

"Leo Tan Creti?" The name had been in the headlines. "That's the guy who is behind all this?" He had detected the frustration in her voice. "I can't take him out alone. I need your help."

"I dropped my gun when the hitman grabbed me on the porch."

"Okay, that makes it a little harder," Landon conceded, "but it's still two against one, and I have my gun."

"I don't think he had a handgun, or he would have used it on me by now. That means there are two of us and we have one gun." She seemed to be coming back to life, engaging with the plan he'd proposed. "He might be desperate for money and that's why he opted to come into the house and try to get at me."

"Guess you have a lot of experience with how these guys operate."

Natasha turned to look at him. "More than I ever wanted to know."

He sensed the anguish behind those words. "I'll ease the car forward with the headlights off. We'll get a close as we can. Maybe we'll catch a break. If the wind would just let up a little, we might have enough visibility to pinpoint the front porch."

"Even if we are able to get into the house," she noted, "we have no idea where he is in there. He was headed up the stairs, where you keep your workout gear, and he has a flashlight, so he can get around."

"You don't think he followed you out onto the roof?"

"Not sure. I doubt it. What I did was super risky," she said. "I had no other choice. If he caught me, he would have killed me." She pulled the blanket away from her chin. "The smart thing to do would be to wait inside until the storm breaks—and I think this guy is smart."

Landon leaned forward and shifted the car into Drive. "Okay, let's do this."

NINE

While Landon moved the car forward at a snail's pace, tension coiled around Natasha's torso like a snake trying to suck the breath out of her. She considered what other options they had. They could sit through the night in the car, running the heater intermittently and trying to stay warm until the storm broke. Trying to drive away with zero visibility meant they would probably end up in a snowbank, making them vulnerable and giving the assassin another opportunity to come after her once the storm broke.

Landon was right. The best option was to try to take the hitman by surprise before he had a chance to escape or to come after her again.

The car bumped against something and Landon eased up on the pedal while the engine idled. "Whatever I hit, it's solid. Last time I hit something the bumper could push against."

"Are you saying it's the porch?"

He rubbed his chin. "Or it could be my truck or the trooper SUV. If it is, I know where we are in relationship to the house. It's only about ten feet to get to the front steps from where those vehicles are parked."

"Yeah, but from what I understand about whiteouts like this, it's easy to lose your sense of direction. It happened to me when I jumped off the porch roof." She fought hard to purge the fear from her voice.

"I can't do this alone, Natasha," Landon said. "I wish I could. I know you're afraid, so am I."

She took in a deep breath. "Tell me what the strategy is."

"We need to get out of the car together, holding hands. You cannot let go of me, no matter what. We need to keep our other hand on the car until it connects with whatever we have butted up against."

"Okay." She zipped her coat up to the neck and secured the hood over her head. "Do you want your glove back?"

"No, keep it. Open the glove compartment. I have some leather driving gloves in there. That will least give me a little coverage if not as much warmth as a winter glove."

She complied and handed him the gloves. He picked the one he needed and slipped it on his hand. "Let's go on the passenger-side door."

Natasha straightened in her seat, tore off the blanket and clicked the door open before grabbing his hand. The wind hit her immediately as she placed her foot on the ground. She waited for Landon to move across the seat, then pushed the door open even wider and set her other foot on the ground. She squeezed his hand as she got to her feet.

She reached out for the hood of the car with her free hand. The sound of the car door slamming shut reached her ears as she edged forward. She bent her head, trying to shut out some of the driving snow as her hand patted along the hood of the car.

Landon's grip on her other hand remained tight. She got to the end of the hood and reached out, trying to feel whatever object they had butted up against. Her hand touched the metal of a truck bed.

She turned back to Landon. Though their heads were only inches apart, she felt like she had to shout to be heard above the shrill and gusting wind. "It's your truck."

He leaned even closer to her. "Feel your way around it to the other side. When you get to the front headlight, look down. There should be paving stones that lead to the front porch."

She squeezed his hand to let him know she understood and then placed her palm on the bed of the truck and felt along until she touched the rear bumper.

The cold had begun to seep into her skin as she pressed her hip against the back bumper and slid along it, her free hand touching the tailgate.

With the wind and cold howling and swirling around them, she navigated by touch to the front headlight. She opened her eyes and looked down. Nothing but white. Then she saw her boot and a paving stone. She took a step forward.

The stones led to the first step of the porch. Still holding her hand, Landon came to stand beside her, and they moved up step by step. Once they were beneath the shelter of the porch, she could see the door, the beige siding on the house and a dark window.

Landon pulled her close so he could speak into her ear. "He might be waiting for us. Assuming that we will try to come back inside. I'll go in first. Stay close."

Landon stepped across the porch and then knelt and eased the door open. She slipped inside after him, letting go of his hand to do so. She followed close behind him, crawling on all fours until she reached out to touch his leg where he was leaning against a wall. She slipped in beside him. His shoulder pressed against hers. She heard him exhale softly.

In the darkness, Natasha tuned her ears to the sounds around her. The house, or maybe it was the glass in the windows, creaked from the wind hitting it. She heard another sound she could not identify. It was too repetitive to be human, as sort of crackling crunching noise.

They sat in the darkness for at least ten minutes.

She heard no footsteps or any sound that might indicate where the assassin might be. Landon's theory that he would not leave the safety of the house until a break in the storm was the most likely scenario, especially if he thought they were outside freezing to death.

If the hitman had been anywhere close, he would have heard the door easing open, even though Landon had been very quiet. In a still house like this, any out of place noise would have raised suspicion and the assassin would have come into the entryway to at least make sure he was still alone.

Crawling on hands and knees, Landon moved forward through the kitchen toward the living room. As she eased around the counters and entered the living room, Natasha saw the source of the crinkling noise. Flames danced in the window of the woodstove. The assassin must have put more logs on the fire to keep the house warm. Still, there was no sign of him.

Landon pressed his back against the wall facing the

woodstove. He tugged on her sleeve, indicating that she should do the same. As she got into position, she could hear and feel him moving around. He pulled his gun from the holster.

He leaned close to her and whispered, "Sooner or later, he'll make noise. It will tell us where in the house he is."

So their strategy was to wait. Except for the little bit of light from the flames in the window of the woodstove, they were in total darkness. She could barely discern the outline of the furniture.

They waited for what seemed like an hour, though she could not be sure. Her eyelids grew heavy and she slept for short periods, waking with a start. Landon remained close. Nothing had changed.

A single thudding noise came from the other end of the house.

Though she remained still, her heart pounded.

Landon still did not move. "That might have been snow sliding off the roof. Let's wait." He'd put his mouth very close to her ear to whisper.

With her heartbeat thrumming in her ears, she stared across the living room toward the woodstove. Her body stiffened. There had been a lump by the overstuffed chair positioned at a side angle from the stove. The lump was no longer there.

Blood froze in her veins.

"I think he's in this room, and he's moving toward us."

Landon tightened his grip on the gun. He dare not even whisper because it would give away their position if the assassin was indeed in the dark room. They may have made a fatal error in talking in the first place.

Adrenaline coursed through him as he tried to discern shapes in the room. The man must be inching toward them silently.

Natasha leaned her shoulder with more pressure against his to get his attention. She lifted her hand. Though he could not be sure, it looked as though she was pointing not too far from the chair by the fireplace.

He studied the area for a long moment. Sweat trickled down his back and his mouth went dry. It wasn't so much that he saw movement but that he sensed the other person in the room.

He could not see well enough to take an accurate shot. At this point, he wanted to take the man in alive so he could be questioned. The man must be moving an inch every five minutes. He had probably been sitting in front of the fire and had heard them come in. He'd then likely crouched beside the chair, knowing the darkness would hide him.

This felt like a game of slow-motion chicken. Who would blink first? Who would try to attack first?

The assassin must still be operating under the assumption that they had not detected him yet.

The best strategy would be to run to another hiding place, hoping the guy moved loudly enough or that the minimal light provided enough of a view for Landon to get off a decent shot.

He wasn't sure how to communicate that to Natasha without talking or moving in a way that might make a sound. They'd made noise when they'd first entered the living room and their whispering had probably given away their approximate location.

He pressed his elbow against Natasha's side, hoping she would understand. He cringed. His ski coat rubbing against hers made a tiny scratching noise. He hoped it sounded like the creaking of the house as wind hit the outside.

Natasha seemed to understand what he was saying. She eased away from him and then took off. He could hear her crawling as the flooring changed from the carpet of the living room to the linoleum of the kitchen.

Landon swung around, his weapon aimed, expecting to hear footsteps headed for Natasha. Instead only silence pressed on his eardrums.

His breathing became more labored as he adjusted the grip on his gun. He was aware that any noise could give away his exact location. In the kitchen, Natasha had become quiet, as well. Maybe she was waiting for him. There was no way he could communicate the nuances of his plan without talking. She was smart woman with honed survival skills. He had to trust that she knew how to keep herself safe.

Natasha was the primary target, but the assassin would take Landon out to get to her. He was still in a sitting position with his back against the wall. It was so quiet that if the hitman took even one step toward the kitchen, Landon was sure he would hear it.

The man might still be moving on his belly, which would be harder to detect.

The seconds ticked by. He listened.

The plan was not working as he'd hoped. The assailant was not giving himself away so easily.

Because it was so quiet, even the smallest noise seemed augmented. Outside, the storm continued to howl and wail. The flames behind the woodstove window were the only things that broke up the blackness.

Landon heard a single soft thud before a body was

on top of him. His gun went off, sending a bullet into the roof. The assassin pinned him to the floor and grabbed at the hand that held the gun.

Landon jerked his hand away, still gripping the gun. The two men struggled for possession of the weapon. Landon tossed the semiautomatic, knowing that it would be impossible to find in the dark, a better option than letting the hired gun get it. The man angled his body slightly and lifted his head when the gun hit the floor. He was probably trying to figure out where it had landed. The momentary distraction gave Landon the opportunity he needed. He punched the assassin hard in the stomach and then landed another blow to his face.

The move only seemed to fuel the assassin's anger. He pummeled Landon with blows to the head and neck, and then sent a hard fist into Landon's solar plexus, which took his breath away. He wheezed. This man knew how to kill with his hands. Another blow like that and Landon would be a goner. As it was, it felt like he was breathing through a straw.

Noise behind him alerted Landon that Natasha had jumped into the fray. Something collided with the hitman's head. And then there was another blow and a muffled grunt, indicating the man was in some pain. In an effort to get away before he was hit again, the man rolled off Landon. There was another groan of pain. Landon wondered what Natasha had used as a weapon.

Landon turned sideways, still trying to get his wind back. He reached out for where he thought the man had rolled but grasped only air.

He heard retreating footsteps. Someone was scrambling across the floor. He pushed himself to his feet, swaying slightly as everything fell silent again. He reached out into the darkness. No one was close. And there was no sound of a struggle.

Maybe Natasha had gotten to a hiding place before she could be attacked.

His own breathing seemed to get louder as he stood, listening for some clue as to what had happened. He didn't think the hitman was in the room anymore. Nor did he sense that anyone was close by. But he couldn't be sure. The guy had proved already that he had some stealth skills.

Landon turned and faced toward the kitchen, taking a single step and then waiting before taking another one.

He felt a hand slip into his. Delicate fingers squeezed his callused hand. She had found him in the dark without making a noise or giving herself away.

He squeezed her hand back. Again, they stood in the dark, waiting and listening for a long moment. Satisfied that the assailant had left the room, he leaned close and whispered, "We need to find the gun."

Both of them dropped to the floor. He swept his hand an inch above the carpet aware that any noise might give them away if the hitman was just waiting around the corner. It seemed odd that he would retreat and not come back.

Natasha stayed close to him but covered a different area of the rug. When they were within ten feet of the woodstove, his hand brushed over cold metal. He'd found the gun! Now to figure out what had happened to the assassin.

TEN

Natasha sat back on her heels as quietly as possible. Landon scooted close enough to her that she could feel his body heat.

Where had assassin gone? He must have slipped into another room, but why? Was he setting up some sort of trap?

Landon tugged on her sleeve and again they crawled through the dark house. He was probably leading her to a hiding place. The hitman may have moved around the corner or even down the hallway.

Landon led her to an alcove off to the side of the woodstove and far away from any light that might come through the sliding glass doors that led to the back porch where they had gotten wood for the fire. They settled in a corner, their shoulders touching.

She brought her knees up to her chest. Her mind was spinning as to why the assassin hadn't come after them yet. The silence and the bracing for the next attack was almost worse than the fighting.

They waited. She thought he heard noise down the hallway but couldn't be sure. Despite the level of adrenaline coursing through her body, Natasha found herself nodding off, waking and falling asleep again. Landon remained close to her and alert.

He roused her awake and she opened her eyes. Though the little alcove was still covered in shadows, it looked like some light was streaming into the rest of the room.

They crawled out together. Though it was still snowing, the wind was not as intense. A ray of sunshine snuck through the sliding glass doors. Landon pulled his phone from his back pocket and quickly put it away. No signal. Still no way to call for help.

Natasha glanced all around the living room. Dark stains on the beige carpet caught her attention. Blood. The bronze sculpture she had hit the man with was on the floor. The piece had sharp points that might have punctured the guy's skin when she'd hit him the second time.

The blood was probably the hitman's. He'd been hurt bad enough to find a place to hole up instead of attacking them again.

She tilted her head, listening for any distinct noise above her or off to the side in the rooms down the hallway.

None of the lights was on, which meant the electricity was still out. But the daylight meant they would be that much easier to find.

Landon slipped back into the alcove and took a position beside her. He spoke in a hushed tone. "It's only been light for a few minutes. Even if he's injured, the road won't be plowed yet, so trying to get out of here by car would still be impossible."

"So he's still in the house?" Her heart beat a little faster.

"It looks like there is some visibility out there. The storm is dying down."

"You think he might try to leave?"

"I don't know how badly he's hurt. It looks like he's lost a lot of blood. He's been so relentless up to this point."

She fought off the terror that encroached on her. They had to be proactive. "He left a blood trail. What if we try to figure out where he is before he has a chance to escape?"

"You're right," Landon said. "There won't be a better time. We have the gun. There are two of us, and he's injured. Depending on where he's holed up, we might be able to take him. On my say-so, if I think it's too dangerous, we find a hiding place and wait him out."

Natasha shook her head. "Agreed."

"Let's head down the hallway. Follow the blood trail. I move in first, to clear the room."

"Okay." She took a deep breath to try to shake off some of the tension that had taken up residence in her chest. Because there were no windows, the light in the hallway was much dimmer than in the living room.

Landon pressed his back against the wall and edged forward.

At first, the blood drops were large enough to see easily. He stopped outside the first room, the one that his late wife's craft stuff was stored in.

She leaned close and whispered, "It looks like the blood trail leads toward the bathroom."

He nodded but then eased open the door to the craft room. He peered inside and then quickly pressed back against the wall on the other side of the door.

If the assailant had been in there and been conscious, he would have jumped Landon.

They worked their way down the hall to the bathroom, where the door was open. The blood trail was easy enough to see on the white linoleum.

Landon peered inside and then edged into the room, still pressed against the wall. While she waited outside, watching, she heard him pull the shower curtain back.

He shout-whispered, "Clear. But he has been in here." He came back out, holding a blood-stained towel. "He's bleeding pretty bad."

Natasha's gaze traveled up the stairs to where Landon had kept his workout gear. Now it was scattered in the hallway.

Landon shook his head. "If he is up there, we'd be too easy a target on those stairs."

As stealthy as the hitman was, she was pretty sure they would have heard him if he'd slipped back into the kitchen. That left them just one room on the other side of the hall, which, she assumed, must be where Landon slept.

Landon pointed, indicating that they needed to clear that room. With a quick glance up the stairs, he moved to the other side of the hallway. The speed at which he moved into the bedroom indicated he thought the man was not hiding in there. He stepped back out and shook his head.

She stared down the hall to just beyond the breaker box. There was no side door the guy could have slipped out through. She angled her upper body so she had a view of the top of the stairs. She could discern the silhouette of the love seat pushed off to one side. No noise came from upstairs. He must have gone up there. But had he slipped out the window once the storm broke or was he still up there?

The assailant was nursing an injury. He'd lost some blood. Would he try to climb out on the roof like she had and escape to wherever he'd left his car? The storm had died down enough that he might have done that. He'd have to dig himself out in a weakened state and then wait for the roads to clear.

A muffled mechanical hum coming from outside caused both of them to run toward the kitchen.

Landon stood off to one side and peered out the window beside the door that led to the porch. She took up a position on the other side of the window. Though the wind was still gusting, she could see most of the front yard. A snowmobile emerged from the garage. The rider was hunched over the handlebars. He sped down the snowy road with relative ease, rounding a curve and disappearing.

Landon shook his head. "That snowmobile wasn't running, or I would have used it to get us out of here. He must have fixed it."

"So now we just wait for the plows." A chill ran down her spine. The assassin had judged that he was in no condition to take them on and had found a way to leave. They had no way to communicate with anyone as long as the cell service was out.

"We don't have a lot of choice here, Natasha. If we tried to take the car or SUV out, we'd just get stuck."

"I get that. It's just that we might have taken one assassin out of commission but once he gets to a place where he can communicate with the man who hired him, someone else will be after me." She turned and looked at him. "We're still trapped here."

* * *

Landon could feel his own agitation rising as Natasha expressed her fear. "It will take him some time to get to the main road and then to town, where the phones might be working. Plus, he's injured." Though he intended his voice to sound calming, he couldn't hide his own concern.

"He used both a handgun and a rifle. Maybe he just went back to his car to get his rifle. He'll pick us off as soon as we step outside."

Her theory held some water. Maybe the assassin wasn't strong enough to risk hand-to-hand combat but could still shoot from a distance. "First things first," he said. "That fire is dead. We need to keep this place warm, and then we'll come up with a plan."

He knew that doing something physical would help to ease the tension he felt and to clear his head. Besides, the house was starting to feel quite chilly. He walked across the living room and pushed open the sliding glass door.

The temperature must be hovering around zero. At least the snow wasn't pelting him. Before he had even placed the first log in the crook of his elbow, Natasha was beside him.

She held her arms out, bent slightly at the elbows. "Why don't you load me up first? The less we have to come outside, the better."

He obliged and then filled his own arms, as well.

Natasha was kneeling by the woodstove with the door open when he came inside. "Looks like there are still some embers in here."

"I can get it going." He knelt beside her after grabbing some sticks and dryer lint from the kindling box. He struck a match to the kindling.

Natasha had risen to her feet. She walked through the living room and pulled all the curtains. "I know it makes it darker in here, but we're not the target of a sniper if he can't see us through the windows." He heard her feet pad across the carpet onto the linoleum and the sound the of kitchen curtains being pulled shut, as well.

She returned and stood at the edge of the living room. "I know what is strange about this house. You don't have any Christmas decorations other than the Christmas card on the refrigerator."

"The card is from my sister." Landon placed several small logs on top of the blazing kindling. How did he explain to her that he hadn't felt like celebrating Christmas since Maggie died? Christmas Eve service was still powerful for him, and he looked forward to it, but no matter how much he wanted to, dragging the decorations out of storage alone had just been too hard. It had always been something he and Maggie had done together.

Natasha walked across the room and sat beside him on the carpet. "Look, it's better that you don't know all the details of my story, and reliving them isn't my idea of a good time." She glanced at him and then at the fire. "There is one thing I want you to know." Her voice wavered and then she took in a breath. "Years before all this bad stuff happened with Leo Tan Creti, I was married, too." She reached out, touched his hand for just a second, and then stared at the dancing flames. "He was shot in the line of duty. I understand why you didn't want to take out the decorations."

"*4 for 4*" MINI-SURVEY

We are prepared to **REWARD** you with 4 FREE Books and Free Gifts for completing our MINI SURVEY!

Romance

Suspense

You'll get up to...

4 FREE BOOKS & FREE GIFTS

FREE Value Over **$20!**

just for participating in our Mini Survey!

Get Up To 4 Free Books!

Dear Reader,

IT'S A FACT: if you answer 4 quick questions, we'll send you 4 FREE REWARDS from each series you try!

Try **Love Inspired® Romance Larger-Print** books and fall in love with inspirational romances that take you on an uplifting journey of faith, forgiveness and hope.

Try **Love Inspired® Suspense Larger-Print** books where courage and optimism unite in stories of faith and love in the face of danger.

Or **TRY BOTH!**

I'm not kidding you. As a leading publisher of women's fiction, we value your opinions... and your time. That's why we are prepared to reward you handsomely for completing our mini-survey. In fact, we have 4 Free Rewards for you, including 2 free books and 2 free gifts from each series you try!

Thank you for participating in our survey,

Pam Powers

To get your 4 FREE REWARDS:
Complete the survey below and return the insert today to receive up to 4 FREE BOOKS and FREE GIFTS guaranteed!

"4 for 4" MINI-SURVEY

1 Is reading one of your favorite hobbies?
☐ YES   ☐ NO

2 Do you prefer to read instead of watch TV?
☐ YES   ☐ NO

3 Do you read newspapers and magazines?
☐ YES   ☐ NO

4 Do you enjoy trying new book series with FREE BOOKS?
☐ YES   ☐ NO

Please send me my Free Rewards, consisting of **2 Free Books from each series I select** and **Free Mystery Gifts**. I understand that I am under no obligation to buy anything, as explained on the back of this card.

❏ **Love Inspired® Romance Larger-Print** (122/322 IDL GQ5X)
❏ **Love Inspired® Suspense Larger-Print** (107/307 IDL GQ5X)
❏ **Try Both** (122/322 & 107/307 IDL GQ6A)

FIRST NAME	LAST NAME

ADDRESS

APT.#	CITY

STATE/PROV.	ZIP/POSTAL CODE

EMAIL ❏   Please check this box if you would like to receive newsletters and promotional emails from Harlequin Enterprises ULC and its affiliates. You can unsubscribe anytime.

LI/SLI-520-MS20

HARLEQUIN READER SERVICE—Here's how it works:

▲ If offer card is missing write to: Harlequin Reader Service, P.O. Box 1341, Buffalo, NY 14240-8531 or visit www.ReaderService.com ▲

BUSINESS REPLY MAIL
FIRST-CLASS MAIL   PERMIT NO. 717   BUFFALO, NY

POSTAGE WILL BE PAID BY ADDRESSEE

HARLEQUIN READER SERVICE
PO BOX 1341
BUFFALO NY 14240-8571

NO POSTAGE
NECESSARY
IF MAILED
IN THE
UNITED STATES

A comfortable silence fell between them as he listened to the crackling of the fire. It was the first time since Maggie's death that he'd felt his heart opening up to a woman. And she would probably be out of his life and into a new one in a matter of days. He shook his head at the irony.

"What are you thinking?" Her voice held a note of playfulness.

"Nothing." All the times he'd eaten at the diner, he had just thought of her as the quiet, efficient waitress. Now he understood why she had always put out a vibe that communicated she wasn't interested in getting to know him better. She'd had to do that to protect who she really was.

"I think it's probably a little more than nothing." Her voice still held that light teasing quality. "No pressure. You don't have to say."

"I was just thinking that sometimes you don't really know a person. It's so easy to make a snap judgment." He rose. He had had a year to get to know Natasha, and now he'd lost his opportunity just when he felt a connection to her. After Maggie's death, women from church had showed an interest in him. Despite their kindness, he had not felt even a spark of attraction.

The brightness he'd noticed in Natasha's features seemed to fall away and her expression became serious. "We need to come up with a plan to stay safe until we're plowed out. Just in case."

"Yes, of course. We'll keep a lookout for anyone approaching. Why don't you watch the back entrance? That way you can stay close to the fire. I'm going to head upstairs. If anyone approaches from the road or surrounding trees, I'll see them coming. If he does come back, I should be able to hear the snowmobile."

She stood, as well. "Back to business." The levity he'd heard in her voice a moment before was gone. She walked toward the glass door with the drawn curtains, pulling them back a few inches to check before sitting the chair by the fire.

Landon headed down the hall and up the stairs. He scooted the love seat over so he could sit in it and watch the driveway but not be seen from below. The snow was now coming down in soft whirling clouds. He could see to the end of his driveway and even some of the road that led to his house. He was bone-weary but he fought his fatigue and tried to stay focused.

The plows always cleared the main roads first. Assuming all the plows were kept running through the night, he estimated it would take at least four to five hours before they got to the secondary roads like the one that led to his house and the other homes in the area.

He nodded off momentarily. A noise caused him to startle awake. He turned around to see Natasha standing beside the love seat, holding a plate of food. "Thought you might be hungry. I opened a couple of cans and rummaged through some cupboards. I'm having a hard time staying awake down there. There is an old saying that food is the same as sleep. Not sure if it's true or not."

He stood and reached out for the plate. "Thanks."

She met his gaze for a moment and then hurried back down the stairs. He stared at the crackers and beans. She'd also placed a cup on the plate that was filled with canned peaches. As he ate and stared out the window, he felt himself perking up. As much as he needed sleep, he knew they both needed to remain alert. Still watching through the window, he finished the meal and set the plate on the floor.

As he settled in for the long vigil ahead, he found his thoughts wandering to Natasha and how she was doing downstairs. It would be so much easier to pass the time if they were together. Despite the dangerous circumstances that had thrown them together, she was an easy person to be with. He stared out the window, surveying the view in front of him by sectors, looking for any change that might indicate they were under siege again. He prayed that the only thing he would see coming up the road would be a plow.

Three hours passed. He straightened and leaned toward the window. He'd spotted a flash of movement in the evergreens lining the road leading to his house. Or at least he thought he had, but he couldn't be sure. It might just be a deer. He was still wound pretty tight. The attacker had been so relentless up to this point, Landon was having a hard time believing the hired gun would just give up even if he was injured. That thought made him sit even straighter. He had to assume they were still under threat.

ELEVEN

Before settling down in the chair by the fire, Natasha made the decision to open the curtains a little wider, so she had a full view of the trees in the backyard. Though it wasn't visible through the trees, Landon had said there was a road behind his house. With the curtains open, she would be able to spot someone coming. But that also meant she was more of a target if the hitman settled in with his rifle. She'd taken every precaution she could think of to keep watch of her surrounding but not be shot at. She'd scooted the chair farther back so it would not be visible from the window.

With the electricity still out, the darkness in the house worked in her favor. Most important, she remained very still in the chair, knowing that someone with sniper skills was attracted to even the slightest movement.

She stared out at the trees, memorizing every shadow and every branch. The warmth from the fire made her drowsy, but she forced herself to stay awake. The days were so short, in another four or five hours, it would start to grow dark again.

Though the snow continued to fall, the wind had

mostly died down. Everything about the scene through the window should have made her feel peaceful, but instead tension twisted inside her.

She jumped up at the sound of footsteps coming down the wooden stairs. She turned quickly, heart racing. Of course, it was a Landon.

"Sorry, I didn't mean to scare you," he said. "I opened the window to get some fresh air to try to stay awake. I think I heard a plow."

She rested a palm over her heart, which was still pounding. "But you are not sure if it is a plow? It could be a snowmobile."

"Agreed. Maybe I was just imagining noises. I'm just wondering if you could give me a second opinion. I'll keep watch down here."

"Okay." She stepped toward him.

He was as on edge as she was. She could hear it in his voice. She hurried along the hall and up the stairs into the room. She leaned toward the window and twisted the latch, then settled on the love seat so she'd be in the shadows. She was still as a statue for a long moment, hearing only her own breathing.

When she held her breath and closed her eyes, she could hear a sort of mechanical humming. So faint, it was almost indistinct from other outside noises such as the almost calm wind and the distant creaking of tree branches.

Something was definitely out there. The noise could just as easily be a snowmobile as a plow. Whatever it was, it was still far away but growing louder.

Landon shouted from the bottom of the stairs. "Do you hear it?"

"Yes," she said.

"So, I'm not going crazy," he said. "I think we need to find a hiding place until we're sure it's a plow."

She rose from her seat with a backward glance, still nothing had come into view. She stared down the stairs. It was so dark that she couldn't see Landon's face clearly. "What do you suggest?"

"If it is the hitman returning, he'll probably check the house first. There is a place we can hide in the shop."

She hurried down the stairs, zipping her coat up. It took them only minutes to find hats and gloves. They stepped outside and off the porch.

She gazed out at the dark landscape. The pristine white snow created a reflective illumination. "It seems like we should see lights by now." Whatever it was would have to come to the top of the hill before they would be able to see it.

"With the mountains all around us, sound sometimes echoes. Even if it is the plows, they could still be out on the main road," he said.

They stepped through several drifts. Both the SUV, the truck and the car were half concealed by snow. The shop's sliding door was still wide open, and snow had blown in front of it, as well.

Landon glanced nervously toward the road. "We can't close this door, or he'll know something is up. I'll keep watch. Why don't you find a hiding place?"

Natasha stared into the dark shop. It didn't look like there was a back door. So the only way in and out was through the two doors on the front. The one that allowed Landon to park his car inside and the other people-size door.

He handed her his flashlight. "So you can get around. Lots of hazards back there."

She took the flashlight and shone it toward the back of the shop. She saw now that Landon must be a woodworker. There was an assortment of saws and hand tools as well as a chair that looked like it needed only to be sanded and finished. She noticed a beautiful cedar box. When she stepped closer, the flashlight revealed that everything was covered in dust. It had been some time since he'd been out here working.

She crouched behind a workbench and clicked off the flashlight. She closed her eyes. The faint mechanical sound seemed to be getting louder, though it would fade out all together from time to time. The noise could be because the plow was working its way along the winding roads or, like Landon had suggested, it was just an echo.

The sound of Landon's pacing reached her ears; his boots scuffing over the concrete.

Her legs were getting stiff. She stood and stretched and then sat again, pressing her back against the wall. It seemed that, if it was the snowmobile coming back, it would have arrived by now, even if the hitman was slowed by his injury and the drifted snow.

"I see lights coming this way." Landon's voice held a mixture of excitement and fear.

She rose and hurried to stand beside him where they were covered by shadows but could see through the open sliding door.

Illumination from the headlights danced across the white landscape.

She clenched her jaw and braced for whatever was about to happen.

* * *

Landon peered out as the mechanical hum of the machine drew closer. The lights were too far apart to be a snowmobile. He relaxed and turned his head toward Natasha, who was pressed against his back. "I think we're going to be okay."

"Are you sure?"

"Ninety-nine percent."

The plow approached. Snow tumbled off either side of the bucket, clearing a path leading to the three vehicles. The plow idled and Landon stepped out into the open and waved. The driver got out of the cab. Even in the dim light, Landon recognized the profile of the driver. The red winter cap with the earflaps and the big belly. Earl Standish.

Landon stepped forward. "Boy, am I glad to see you."

"Looks like you've been snowed in for a while," Earl said.

Natasha, Landon noticed, had stayed behind in the shop. She must still be afraid…uncertain if it was safe. Her trust had been so compromised by all that had happened to her.

"I cleared it for you all the way to the main road." Earl turned slightly in the direction he'd just come from and pointed at the three half-buried vehicles. "Wish I had time. I'd help dig you out. But I got a bunch of folks up the road who have been stranded for as long as you have."

"We'll manage," Landon said. "Is the power on in town?"

"Their electricity stayed on through the worst of it. See you in the funny papers." Earl gave Landon a salute and hurried back to the cab of his plow. The big machine made roaring noises as Earl dropped the bucket and continued down the road. His red taillights glowed as he stirred up the snow around the plow.

Landon hurried back to Natasha, who stepped out of the shadows as the plow drew farther away. "We need to get dug out and fast," he said. "We'll take the SUV. It's more of a winter vehicle. I've got two shovels." He grabbed the one that was leaning against the shop and then headed for the porch, where he kept the other one.

By the time he'd grabbed the shovel and made it down the porch stairs, she was already working by the back tire of the SUV to uncover it. They dug out, only the sound of shovels slicing through the snow filling the air. He was keenly aware of how exposed they were. The roads were clear. It would be nothing for the hitman to return and take aim from a distance with his rifle. He might even be able to park around the corner and approach on foot. They needed to hurry.

Natasha spoke breathlessly as she shoveled. "I thought you were going to loan me your car, so I could get out of town. That's why I came here with you, remember."

His shovel sliced through the snow. "Things have changed since then." He turned and dumped the snow away from the vehicle, stopping for a moment to catch his breath and lean on the shovel. "I see how much danger you're in. I can't, in good conscience, just let you go off by yourself."

She kept shoveling, taking only a moment to glance out at the newly cleared road and then at him. "Okay, what is the plan?"

Her response warmed his heart. Maybe she trusted

him just a little bit now after all they'd gone through. "Soon as we get to a place where the phones work, why don't you try to call your contact in the US Marshal's office again. If he can't meet up with you right away, it will just be a matter of hiding out for a while. I know a place that should be safe."

"Where?"

"I have a friend in a village that is a couple hours' flight from here. It's remote, very safe. I will stay with you up until the time I can hand you off to the marshal. You say this marshal is the one you trust. If you want to stay alive, I am asking you to trust me, too." He had cleared the driver's-side door of snow. "Deal?"

She kept shoveling. "Okay."

He opened the driver's door and got in behind the wheel. The SUV had been sitting for a long time in the cold. The battery may have gone dead. He prayed it would start. He turned the key in the ignition. It sputtered. He tensed, and then the motor caught and roared to life.

He let out a heavy breath filled with thanks to God.

When he climbed out of the SUV, Natasha was leaning on the shovel. The winter chill made her breath form puffy clouds as she exhaled. "Don't you have people expecting you for Christmas?"

She must have taken the time to mull over his plan and come up with an objection.

"'Course I do. But they will understand. I've worked the holidays before. I'll just celebrate with my siblings a little late."

"Thank you." Her words were filled with warmth and appreciation. Again, she glanced down the road. Her back stiffened. "As long as I'm in Little Bear, he can find me." Just like that, the hard edge had come back into her voice. "If he's hurt bad, Tan Creti will just line up someone else. It won't stop."

Landon heard the terror in her voice. It didn't seem likely that another hired gun would be close by. But he had to take her word for it. She, more so than him, was aware of the reach and the power of this mafia boss who wanted her dead.

"All I need is time to line up a pilot. I know a guy who might be available. Soon as we can get to a place where I can make a few calls."

"Nobody can know where I'm hiding. Not even the other troopers."

Landon nodded. They finished shoveling out the SUV and got in. Landon switched on the headlights, which lit up the front porch.

She stared at the house. "I'm sorry about dropping your gun. I'm sure it's buried in the snow. I'll pay you back for it."

"We'll deal with it when we need to. I still have a gun." Once he got turned around, he rolled down the freshly plowed road. He pressed on the gas, pushing the SUV to go as fast as he dared. The last thing they needed to do was to slip off the road. He was keenly aware, though, that the hired gun might have hidden in the trees and be waiting for an opportunity to pick them off.

As the cab of the SUV grew warmer, Natasha took her gloves off and unzipped her winter coat halfway.

"Can you do me a favor?" He stared at the dark road ahead.

"Sure."

"Keep checking my phone." He handed it to her. "Let me know when you have a signal."

"I imagine there are not that many towers to ping a signal off around here."

"The closer we get to town, the more likely it is that we'll be able to get a signal."

She looked at the phone and then placed it in her lap just as they arrived at the main road. Judging from the piles of either side of the road, they must have had close to a foot of snow.

The only other vehicle they passed on their way toward town was a plow headed in the opposite direction.

Landon rounded a curve. As they approached the Kodiak Diner, he saw that it was dark and that there were no cars in the parking lot.

She placed her hand on the window as they drove past. "I'm going to miss that place…and the people I worked with."

"You did a good thing saving Ezra from his erratic dad."

"I hope things turn out good for him and his mom and grandma. They are good people."

"Must be hard leaving people behind…over and over."

She nodded.

When Maggie had died, he'd felt like a vital organ had been ripped from his body and he'd been told he had to live anyway. It was probably the same for Natasha, only she had to keep on doing it, losing everything that mattered.

They drove several more minutes until he could see the lights of Little Bear in the distance as well as the light of some of the homes and businesses that were outside the city limits. They hadn't been attacked again, maybe the hitman had gone into town for medical care.

Natasha checked his phone. "I have a signal. I'll see if I can reach Marshal Henderson." She pressed in the memorized number. It rang twice. Static and a very faint "Hello?" came across the line.

He must be in place with a bad signal. All the same, it was good to hear his voice.

"Walter, it's Natasha Hale. I need to be moved ASAP."

"What happened?"

"Tan Creti sent an assassin. My face was on the news. That's how they found me."

The marshal's voice was breaking up. "That is serious. We have limited administration over the holidays, and I am still up north. If you would be open to another marshal helping you…?"

"I don't want to do that, Walter. I'm concerned about info being leaked to Tan Creti or him being able to buy someone off. We know there is a leak somewhere down the line because Tan Creti found me the first time I was given a new identity."

"I get it. If you can meet me in Anchorage, I can get you to a safe house on December 26."

"I can do that."

"I will get in touch with you about the exact meeting place…on this cell number." Walter's voice warbled. "Can you stay safe until then?"

"I think so. I am with a trooper who is helping me. I trust him." Natasha glanced over at Landon. The words echoed through her head, and she knew it was true.

"…be in touch."

The line went dead.

"So?" Landon stared through the windshield. Snow was piled up on either side of the road.

"He can't make it happen until after Christmas."

"Okay, I guess we go with plan B—we get hold of my friend."

He pulled over into the parking lot of a convenience store on the edge of town. The lights were on inside, creating a warm glow. A lone clerk stood behind the counter. There was only one other car in the parking lot.

Landon reached his hand out for his phone. She handed it to him, and he pressed in some numbers.

Natasha glanced around, taking note of her surroundings.

His phone rang. He looked in the rearview mirror, watching a car ease along on the road leading into town. It slowed as it passed the convenience store. They were somewhat conspicuous in the trooper vehicle.

Natasha's voice filled with tension. "I think we need to park somewhere else."

TWELVE

Natasha craned her neck and peered out the window at the slow-moving car. It never sped up and then it slipped out of sight down a hill headed toward town. She tensed, feeling a knot in her stomach. Maybe that was the man who wanted to kill her. The car he'd been driving was very generic and dark in color. It was possible he was looking for a place to turn around and come back this way. It could also just be a curious onlooker. They couldn't take a chance.

"Hey, Ted." Landon's pilot friend must have picked up. Landon glanced over at her and then spoke into the phone. "Can you hold on for just a second?" He handed her the phone and shifted into Reverse. "If you could talk to him and tell him what we need, that would be great."

Landon pulled out of the lot, turned down a residential street and kept driving.

"Ted," she said, "this is Natasha. I'm a friend of Landon's. We need to charter your plane as soon as possible."

"That might be a possibility," Ted responded, "it

depends on where you're going. This storm is still affecting parts of the state, and flying is not a good idea."

Her spirits sank. If they couldn't escape by plane, what were they going to do?

Ted piped up. "Where is it you wanted to go?"

She pulled the phone away from her ear and addressed Landon. "What's the name of the place we need go?"

"Pirta Bay," he told her.

She repeated the village name into the phone.

"Just a second," Ted said. "Let me check the conditions in that direction." She heard the sound of Ted typing on a keyboard.

Her stomach tied into a knot. If they couldn't get out by plane, that left driving. Many of the roads probably still weren't cleared, and they were way more vulnerable in a car. Alaska really didn't have much of a highway system.

Landon pulled onto another residential street and then turned down an alley where no one would be able to spot them.

"Thank you." She handed him back the phone and listened to the one-sided conversation.

"Hey, Ted, it's me on the line… Okay… Two hours… Sure we can be there. See you then."

She breathed a sigh of relief. "He can take us?"

Landon clicked off the phone. "He'll meet us at the marina where Gary was caught. We've got some time. We need to go to the store and get some things. There is not much in the village. Their supplies are brought in by plane."

"I have supplies back at my house in my car," she said.

"Best to stay where there are people, don't you

think? Besides, what if the road to your house isn't plowed yet? The last thing we want to do is get stuck in the middle of nowhere when we have flight to catch."

The truth was, whether she was in a crowd or by herself, Natasha never completely dropped her guard. All the same, she nodded. "Okay."

Landon turned the SUV back on and rolled down the alley. "Also, I want to have a trooper check out the ER to see if a wounded man came in there. We don't know how badly he was hurt."

"We don't know what he looks like or even exactly where he was hurt. People could have been wounded for other reasons?"

"All the same, procedurally. I need to cover all the bases."

Even though Landon was taking every step possible to ensure her safety, she could not let go of the fear that made her stomach tighten.

"I need to see if anybody reported finding my snow-mobile. He probably left it by wherever he hid his car, but we still need to check it out. If we could get this guy in custody, it would go a long way in keeping you safe, even if the mafia can line up someone else."

As Landon entered the city limits, he noted that some of the places were still dark and the streets un-plowed. He clicked his blinker and turned into a lot by a store that was both a hardware and grocery store. Like so many places in a small town, Wilhelm's Market served a dual purpose. He didn't park in front. Instead, he found a parking space at the side of the building where the employees probably parked.

"Let me call to send a trooper over to the hospital first before we go inside," he said.

She rubbed her hand on her thigh and took in a deep breath, trying to release some of the tension building up in her body.

Landon pressed in a number and glanced over at her. "It's a small hospital. Like, twelve beds. If any stranger came in, he would stick out like a sore thumb." He turned his attention back to the phone and gave the other trooper instructions.

She was glad that Landon was trying to get the guy in custody.

Landon clicked off his phone. "One more call," he said.

She listened while he called his friend in Pirta Bay to let him know he was coming. She gathered that his name was Mitch.

Landon ended the call and looked her way. Her body language must have given away how tense she was. He reached over and squeezed her shoulder. "Just stay close to me in the store. It will be okay."

They got out of the SUV and walked to the front of the store. He opened the door for her and let her enter first. She noticed that he glanced over his shoulder before stepping in behind her. Inside, the young man behind the checkout counter nodded in recognition of Landon. Natasha didn't know him.

The lights in the store seemed unusually bright, she thought as Landon grabbed a cart and directed her toward a food aisle. As they walked, she noticed only two other people in the store besides the clerk.

Many of the shelves were bare.

"Looks like people went into a bit of a panic with the storm," she said.

"We'll find what we can." Landon grabbed the last

box of protein bars. "In addition to some food for us, I like to bring some things to my friend since he doesn't get supplies often. Any little gift I can take is appreciated." Landon loaded in a few more groceries.

They walked past a display of Christmas decorations. The festiveness of the holiday seemed so far away. Knowing that Natasha had no relatives close by, Judy and Betty had invited her to join them for Christmas Day dinner. She had been looking forward to it. As guarded as she needed to remain, the invitation had made her feel less alone and like she was finding her place in Little Bear.

Landon worked his way toward the hardware section of the store. Natasha followed. As they turned the corner, she glanced up to the convex security mirror mounted high on the wall. She saw boots and jeans coming toward them. The footsteps of the man pounded heavily. She turned to see who it was.

"Hey, Landon." An older, fit man was making his way toward them.

Landon held out his hand to the man. "Richard."

"Heard you had some excitement with Gary Tharp." The man looked at Natasha. "You're the waitress from the diner that was involved. Saw it all over the news."

"Yes, that was me." She could feel her face growing hot. Just a reminder that the news story wasn't dead yet. She looked away and then feigned interest in a display of hammers.

"Natasha, Richard is a retired trooper." Landon's tone suggested that he wanted to put her at ease.

She pulled one of the hammers off the rack and glanced back at them. "Pleased to meet you."

"So what are you two up to?"

"This and that," Landon said. "Just trying to recover from the storm. That was a doozy."

Landon's body language suggested a high level of trust toward the older man. She wished she shared his confidence. If Richard used to be in law enforcement, he had some shooting skills. They'd never gotten a good look at the hitman. Landon seemed to understand the importance of not saying they were headed out of town.

She put the hammer back on the hook. "Landon, don't you think we should get going?" Then she looked at Richard. "Storm did a lot of damage to both our places." Her comment was meant to imply that she and Landon were working together on repairs. It was a well-practiced diversionary tactic. She hated the deception, but she knew from experience that it was necessary.

Landon said goodbye, and Richard walked away.

He threw a few more things in his cart. She grabbed a phone for herself. They headed toward the checkout counter. Landon stood close to her as the clerk rang up their items. She shrank back from the big, front display windows, slipping on the other side of Landon and pressing close to him. The windows would be a perfect opportunity for a sniper to shoot at them from the building across the street.

Though they were taking every precaution, Natasha could not let go of her fear. Fear and hyper-vigilance had kept her alive so far.

"Is there a back way for us to get out of here?" she whispered.

"That is for employees only." Landon handed her a bag of purchases, and he grabbed the other.

They hurried outside and got into the SUV. The only way to get back to the main road was to drive through the front lot of the store. As they drove by, she noticed Richard standing in front of the big window. He lifted his hand and waved as they passed. Landon waved back.

"He's a good guy," Landon said.

"We just can't take any chances. The more people who see us together around town, the more likely we are to be tracked down if the guy who's after me starts asking questions."

"A stranger asking questions would send up red flags."

"You said it yourself. He's probably a local guy. It could be Richard," she said.

"I know Alaska is a good place for people who have a past to come and hide. It's possible that Tan Creti called on someone who lives around here." He glanced at the clock on the dashboard. "We've got some time to kill. Since you don't want to be seen, I'll find us a hiding place close to the marina."

"Thank you. I'm sorry to be so on edge."

He drove through town. "It's understandable, but sooner or later, you have to accept that most people aren't out to get you."

"That kind of thinking gets you killed," she said. "The funny thing is that after being here a year, I was starting to let my guard down...to think maybe this would be my home." The intensity of emotion that came out in her voice surprised her.

"I wish this could have been your home, too. Wish I had taken the time to get to know you better."

"Just bad timing, I guess." Marshal Henderson had

advised her that deep romantic attachments were not a good idea. It made it that much harder to pull up stakes. He'd said it was inevitable that if she grew close to someone, she might end up sharing who she really was. And there was always the danger of a former love interest spilling the beans on her real identity. "Another place and another time, huh?"

He took a turn onto the road that led to the marina. More cars were out on the road. "We can park where we have a view of the marina so we can see when my friend lands."

As they drove over the hills that led to the marina, the lake came into view. Landon took another turn down a side road that looked like it hadn't been plowed. "I don't want to get too far down here and get stuck." He brought the SUV to a stop. "We can climb that hill. We will be able to see Ted as he comes in for a landing."

They got out of the vehicle and trekked up the hill. There was a light breeze blowing and the sun was shining. Though she couldn't see the dock where the boats and seaplanes were, the lake had a sparkling-crystal quality. Despite the peaceful landscape, the deep and drifted snow served as evidence of the blizzard.

Landon pulled his phone out. "I'm going to have to call the other troopers to let them know to come out here and get the vehicle." He held up a hand as if to stop her from protesting. "Before you say anything, I know that means the troopers will know that we took off in a plane. They are not going to know where we went. I'll just tell them this is official business, which it kind of is, right?"

"Yes. I understand leaving the vehicle here for too long means it would be vandalized or stolen," she said.

While Landon made his call, she sat and appreciated the peacefulness of the moment, knowing that it wouldn't last. Maybe the guy who had come after them was so injured he was out of commission. That didn't matter. Leo Tan Creti had plenty of hired guns at his disposal. The one thing she knew was that until she had a new identity and place to live, Tan Creti would not give up until she was dead.

THIRTEEN

After he made his call, Landon clicked off the phone and stared down the hill at the lake. A distant buzzing sound in the sky made him sit straighter. He shaded his eyes but still couldn't see anything. "That's probably Ted. His plane is red. Let's wait and make sure. It will only take a few minutes to drive down to the marina."

Both of them watched the sky. The plane became a black dot and the buzz of the engine grew even louder when it dropped lower in the sky.

Natasha stood. "It looks red to me."

"Let's go." They walked down the hill, their boots sinking into the deep snow. A trooper would be along within minutes to pick up the SUV at the marina. Though they had not seen the hitman since he'd left his house, Landon could not shake the sense of urgency that plagued him.

The mafia boss knew that Natasha was in Little Bear. The faster he got her out of here, the better. They got into the SUV and headed for the marina.

Unlike the last time they had been there, the marina was buzzing with activity. Lots of boats may have come in seeking shelter from the storm. A very dif-

ferent picture from before when they were here dealing with Gary. He counted six planes. The parking lot
had seven cars. Though the car the hitman had driven
was utterly generic, none of the vehicles set off alarm
bells for him.

They arrived at the dock just as his friend landed.

Landon parked the SUV and they unloaded the supplies they'd picked up. After checking to make sure no
one was watching, he locked the SUV and placed the
key on the top of the front tire where Russ would find it.

As they carried the supplies along the dock, Ted
waved at them. He stepped toward Landon and Natasha and held out his hands to take Natasha's box of
supplies. "I'm all gassed up and ready to go."

It took them only minutes to get loaded and belted
into their seats. They skimmed across the water and then
lifted up. As they gained altitude, Landon had a view
of the dock below. He saw the SUV with the trooper
insignia on its side arrive. It came to a stop and Russ
got out to walk toward the vehicle Landon had left behind. Deb, the other trooper, must be behind the wheel.

The people, planes, boats and cars grew smaller as
he stared down. Just as the dock slipped out of view,
he saw a man park his car, get out and stare up at them.

Landon's phone rang. It was Russ. "Yes?"

"Just thought you might want to know. There was a
tracking device attached to your trooper vehicle. Just
noticed it under the back bumper."

"Thanks. Good to know." He clicked off his phone.
He'd been deliberate in his word choice, not wanting to
scare Natasha. So they had probably been followed to
the marina. Landon glanced over at Natasha.

She offered him a faint smile, but he noticed she was gripping the armrest. "Flying is not really my thing."

He nodded.

"What was the phone call about?"

"Russ wanted me to know they had gotten the SUV."

From her side of the plane, she did not have a view of the parking lot. Even if it was short-lived, he thought she deserved a brief reprieve that wasn't filled with worry and hyper-vigilance. "We'll be in the air for a couple of hours."

She rested her head against the back of the seat and closed her eyes.

Landon, on the other hand, found his mind racing. So they'd been tracked to the marina. That didn't mean the man after Natasha knew where they were going in the plane. All pilots had to file flight plans before they took off. He didn't know who might have access to that information. Certainly, it wasn't public knowledge. The name of the plane was painted on the side. Natasha had said that Tan Creti had resources and a reach that Landon could not begin to fathom. He had to assume that though it might take some time, they would be tracked to the village.

Natasha's head had tilted to one side, and her breathing had changed. At least she was able to get some rest even if he couldn't.

Natasha was surprised at how deeply she'd slept despite not liking flying. She didn't wake until the plane was bouncing along the water, headed toward a dock.

The plane shook from the impact of hitting the water, rising up and coming down again. Landon stared at her. She saw a softness in his expression and warmth in his eyes.

"Sleep okay?"

She nodded. Through the window, she saw only a fog on the water and the faint outline of houses in the distance. "You can't drive to this place, huh?"

"Plane, dogsled or snowmobile work best," Landon said. "Depending on the time of the year, the roads are pretty iffy."

Landon had said they'd be safe here.

Once the plane was in the dock, they helped Ted unload the stuff he told them he'd brought to sell and trade, along with their own boxes.

Such short days. It was already dark, though it wasn't even dinnertime yet.

The pilot looked up. "Looks like a fog moving in. I'm going to deal with some things and try to get out of here before takeoff becomes impossible."

"Let us help you haul stuff." Landon leaned over to pick up a duffel, and she did the same.

The village of Pirta Bay looked like a series of random houses, many of them trailers, and none of the streets followed a straight line.

Natasha walked beside Landon as they passed several houses that had kennels where dogs were kept. "What does your friend who lives here do?" she asked.

"He's the schoolteacher."

"Oh, a teacher."

"No, he's *the* teacher, all twelve grades."

As they made their way up the winding dirt streets, children and adults playing outside stopped and stared at them and then resumed their activities.

"You folks are just in time for the Christmas program," Ted said. "They usually put on a pretty good feed afterward. Everyone goes. Hopefully, I'll be in the air by then."

"I know about that," Landon said. "Mitch, my friend, is probably the guy in charge. I don't know if we will be going, though."

Natasha wondered why Landon seemed on edge. Hadn't they come here because it was such a hard-to-reach place?

"I got to head off this way," Ted noted.

"Thanks for the lift on such short notice," Landon said.

The pilot veered down what passed for a side street. At the end of the street there was a house with a hand-painted sign that said General Store.

"We can dump our stuff at Mitch's place. He's probably at the school," Landon said.

Mitch's place was a single-wide trailer. Given the transportation challenge, Natasha wondered how they had even gotten the trailer here. She had noticed some stick-built houses, as well. Landon knocked on the door. When there was no answer, he eased it open and shouted, "Mitch, are you home?"

When his inquiry was greeted with only silence, Landon gestured that they go inside. The trailer was tidy. Except for an abundance of books, Mitch seemed to live a very minimalist lifestyle.

"How do you guys know each other?"

"We met at a summer camp my parents sent me to in Montana. A year later, Mitch came up here to visit and fell in love with Alaska. It was always his goal to move here which he did after college. He's been my friend since we were twelve."

"That's a long time to be friends."

"Yeah, we try to plan our vacation time so we can hike or kayak or whatever together. I come up here when I need to get away. Stayed for weeks after Maggie died."

"This place gave you solace?"

"Yes. You can take the dogsled out so far, you don't even see another person. Just quiet for miles." Landon put down the box of supplies.

"So what do we do now?"

"Natasha, I need to tell you something." Landon pressed his lips together. "I doubt the guy who is after you could follow us here directly anyway, but I think he knows we took off in a plane. There was a tracking device on the SUV."

The news hit her like a knife to her heart. Just when she'd thought she could get her breath… "But if he shows up, we'll know. A stranger sticks out like a sore thumb around here. And it would take quite a while for a snowmobile to get here."

Landon nodded. "Mitch doesn't know exactly why I came here, and I think it would be good for him to be in the loop, for extra protection. He can be trusted. Why don't you stay close to me and we'll go find him."

"And then maybe we should hide out here?"

"We'll keep a low profile for sure. The villagers know me, but you are a stranger, so if someone does come around asking questions…"

He opened the door for her and let her go first. They followed a snow-covered but well-worn path. Landon seemed to be choosing side streets where there were no people.

The school was three Quonset huts with enclosed adjoining walkways. It was clear where most of the activity was taking place. Landon and Natasha watched from a distance as people arrived with coolers, casserole dishes and Crock-Pots. Some had costumes slung over their arms, while others carried microphones and sound equipment. Gradually, the activity outside the school died down.

A balding redheaded man came outside, looking one way and then the other.

Landon stepped out of the shadows. "That's Mitch." His expression brightened at the sight of his friend.

Recognition spread across Mitch's face, and he jogged over to Landon and took him into a big bear hug.

Mitch stood back, still smiling, and then turned his attention to Natasha. "This must be your friend." He held out his hand to her. "Sorry I couldn't meet you at the house. We're all hands on deck to pull this thing off." He turned back toward the school. "I know it looks like total chaos, but we've got some pretty talented people, and those that aren't talented are a hoot to watch anyway. Why don't you guys come inside and enjoy?"

Landon's shoulders tensed, nearly touching his ears. "Mitch, I need to explain something to you." Landon summarized the threat that Natasha was under but did not say she was in WITSEC. "Far as we know, no one followed us here."

"And they probably won't, or it will take them a while to show up. I think you are safe for now," Mitch said. "Look, I'm in charge of this whole thing. The show is about to start. The house lights are already down. No one will see you. Safer in a crowd than back at my trailer when the whole village is here." Mitch took off and disappeared inside.

"He's right. We're no safer at the trailer than in the

school. We could at least watch a Christmas show." Back at the plane, when Ted had first mentioned the performance and potluck, she'd found her heart longing to be able to do such a normal holiday thing.

Landon shrugged. "Let's find a place toward the back and leave before we're noticed." They entered the dark room and slipped into the back row, which had only one other person in it.

The stage was set with risers and a manger scene. A kid walked across the floor, escorting a baby goat on a leash, and disappeared backstage. A girl of about eight or nine handed out programs at the door. The curtain opened, and the stage lights intensified. The few people who were talking grew quiet. Just as the first group came on stage, Ted slipped in beside Natasha.

The auditorium had grown so hushed, she dared not even whisper. She assumed that the pilot had been unable to leave due to the fog he'd been hoping to beat.

A spotlight illuminated the middle of the stage. Three preteen children entered. Natasha could see Mitch in the wings, gesturing and running the backstage show. The three children, two girls and a boy, stepped up to the microphone and sang "O Holy Night." Natasha's favorite Christmas carol. The words brought tears to her eyes.

Several more songs were sung by people of different ages. The lyrics of each Christmas carol were like a salve to her heart. Natasha looked over at Landon, whose face was shining, his eyes filled with light.

He glanced sideways, catching her staring at him. Feeling her cheeks warm, she shrugged. His hand slipped into hers. He squeezed her fingers and let go. Somehow, the sense of community created by the performers helped her to capture some of the magic of Christmas that she'd longed for. She wondered if maybe Landon felt the same way.

As the pageant drew to a close, children dressed as Mary and Joseph, wise men, shepherds and angels all came on stage while an older woman stepped up to the microphone and recited the Christmas story from Luke. The goat was led out on stage, as well. The words of the story washed over her, and Natasha felt a deep sense of peace.

The performance ended. After the applause died down, the lights in the auditorium came up and Mitch came out on stage. "Folks, thanks so much for joining us tonight. We have a ton of food set up in the kitchen. You know the routine. Let the children be first in line. Grab your paper plates."

Landon leaned close and whispered in her ear, "Let's get out of here while everyone is thinking about food."

People shuffled around, visiting and hugging.

Natasha gazed up at Landon. The warmth of his smile and the way he gave her arm a friendly squeeze confirmed that she was feeling a bond toward him. Despite how guarded she had been since entering WIT-SEC, she felt her heart opening up to him. Fine, she felt that way. She could acknowledge her growing affection for him without giving in to it.

They both turned their attention toward the pilot.

"So, you didn't make it out on time," Landon said.

"Yeah, the fog came in so fast," Ted said. "Another plane came in just in time."

Natasha's mouth went dry. "Another plane?"

"The guy landed in the fog, showed some real skill.

Another ten minutes and I'm not sure he would have been able to land without some problems."

"Is it someone you know?" Landon's voice remained steady.

"Didn't recognize the pilot or the passenger." He glanced around the room. "I don't see them anywhere around here."

Natasha tried to quell the rising panic. There could be another explanation besides the hitman having followed them. "It is Christmastime. Maybe one of the villagers has a late-arrival relative."

"Yeah, maybe that's it," Landon said. He didn't sound too convincing.

Without a word, Landon wrapped his arm around her and led her to a room off to the side of the stage that appeared to be where the schoolchildren hung their coats and kept their lunches and shoes in cubbies.

She felt like she couldn't get a deep breath. "We don't know anything. It doesn't mean it's him." Was she trying to convince herself of that? Her pounding heart betrayed what she was really thinking.

"Well, from what Ted said, neither the pilot nor his passenger came to this event. My guess is most everyone in the village is here unless they physically couldn't make it."

"We need to find out who that pilot and passenger are."

"Mitch might know if anyone was expecting a visitor. My concern is that the hitman figured out where we went based on me knowing Mitch or he got access to the flight plan. That means they might be waiting at his place."

"How would they find out you knew Mitch?"

"People in town know that I come here. Maybe the guy started asking questions. If he searched my place, he might have found pictures of this place or an envelope with Mitch's address. Who knows?"

The fear she was experiencing seemed to be intensifying by the second. They didn't know anything for sure yet. That's what she had to keep telling herself.

Landon gathered her into his arms and held her close. "You ready for this?"

The comfort of his embrace calmed her. "Guess I have to be, right?"

He held her tighter. "We're in this together, Natasha." He pulled away. His hand brushed her cheek. The soft touch, a reminder of the moment they had shared during the Christmas show. She had had a brief reprieve from a life on the run and a reminder of what really mattered in this world. The birth of a baby in trying circumstances thousands of years ago.

They stepped into the open area where half the people were still visiting and the other half had sat to eat. No one was looking at them.

Her eyes searched his. He probably couldn't explain what they were doing until they were out of earshot of everyone. She would have to trust that he had a plan.

They walked out into the night, zipping their coats against the wall of cold that hit them. It was totally dark. Landon wasn't kidding about the whole village being at the Christmas show. As she looked out at the dark houses and winding makeshift streets, she didn't see any people.

She could not shake the sense of terror that chilled her to the bone.

FOURTEEN

Landon took several steps along the path. He did a continual survey of the area around him.

Natasha kept pace with him. "What are we doing?"

He could hear the fear in her voice.

"First thing, we're going to check out Mitch's place to make sure no one is there waiting for us."

"And then?"

They kept walking, their boots crunching on the dry snow. "I'm not sure. Because of the fog, the only way out of here is by dogsled or snowmobile. Not sure where we will go. If he has followed us here, we can't put the villagers in danger."

"It doesn't make sense to run until we know what we're dealing with," she said.

"It's suspicious to me that neither the pilot nor the passenger has made an appearance at the Christmas potluck. If they knew anyone in this village, it seems like they would have showed up at the dinner."

They turned a corner and Mitch's trailer came into view.

All of the windows in the trailer were dark.

"I would feel better if I had a gun, too," Natasha said.

He'd thought about leaving Natasha back at the

school and doing this himself. It just seemed that the safest place for her to be was with him. "Just stay close to me," he said. "We'll do this together." He unzipped his jacket and pulled his gun out of the holster.

Landon circled the outside of the entire trailer, peering underneath it, while Natasha shone her flashlight at a place where the skirting had come off and someone might be hiding. He moved to the door of the trailer, knowing that it wouldn't be locked. No one in the village locked their doors. "I'll go in first. Wait until I give you the all-clear and you can come in."

He eased the door open and stepped up the two stairs that led inside. The trailer was so dark, it was hard to see anything. He reached for a light switch. Nothing happened. Someone had cut the electricity. He whirled around toward the door where Natasha was on the first step. "Back out. Something is wrong."

He jumped on top of her just as a gunshot broke the silence around them. He couldn't discern where the shot had come from.

Landon rolled off her. "This way." He crawled toward the spot in the trailer where the skirting had been torn off. At least he knew nobody was hiding there. His heart raced as he ushered her under the trailer while he pressed against the side of it with his gun drawn.

Where had the shot come from? The door to the trailer swung on its hinges. Though the sound was distracting, he listened for footfalls from inside. The trailer wasn't on a permanent foundation, the weight of a footstep would make the whole trailer creak.

It seemed a foolish move for the shooter to trap himself inside the trailer.

Landon studied the area around them. Plenty of

places to hide. Yet it didn't seem like the shot had come from there.

In the distance, he heard rising voices and chatter. People were leaving the school and heading to their homes.

He lifted his head as a realization spread through him. The shooter was on the roof of the trailer. He had waited until Landon had gone inside to take aim at Natasha in the split second she was on the steps alone. He had counted on Landon using up time to deal with the electricity not working.

Landon pressed closer to the trailer and then moved to join Natasha. He scrambled to get under the trailer just as another shot was fired. This one had come so close, the percussive boom hurt his ears, though it sounded like the hitman was using some sort of silencing device so as not to alert the villagers.

He pressed close to Natasha. In the silence, he listened for the sound of the shooter moving to get off the roof. If he did that and came after them, they were easy targets. They needed to move out of the hiding place before he could get to them.

The sound of people talking grew louder as they came toward the street where Mitch's trailer was located. The trailer shook slightly. The shooter had jumped off from the other side, maybe scared by the approaching villagers.

A group of maybe eight people walked by the trailer. Laughing and engrossed in their own conversations, they didn't notice Landon and Natasha under the dark trailer. They passed by and turned a corner.

Landon crawled out from under the trailer. "Maybe I

can catch him." He bolted to his feet. "Get in the trailer and lock the door."

He hurried around the side of the trailer, searching every dark corner. There were no streetlights. Most of the houses were still dark. With his weapon drawn, Landon pressed against the side of the nearest dwelling. He heard no pounding footsteps.

He was keenly aware that this might be an ambush. He inched forward, tuning his ears to any noise around him. He could hear people several streets away as they headed back to their houses. Up ahead, in the darkness, he heard a slamming sound like someone bumping into something. He quick-stepped in the direction of the sound. A light flashed and then disappeared. That had to be the hitman using his flashlight to see what was in front of him and then turning it off quickly.

Landon ran as fast as he dared on the uneven terrain. His feet hit a patch of ice. He slid but righted himself. He saw only shadows up ahead.

The hitman was moving farther away from the village and the dwellings. It got even darker. Landon slowed down. There were more silhouettes up ahead. Still holding his gun, he pulled his phone out and clicked on the flashlight app to see what he was dealing with. It appeared to be some storage sheds with piled-up furniture and appliances that probably couldn't be hauled away until spring.

He turned off the flashlight. The hitman could be hiding anywhere, but he couldn't stay there all night. It would get too cold. Raising his gun, Landon took a step forward, drawing close to the first storage shed.

There weren't that many places the guy could run. Landon contemplated alerting the village and doing a search, but didn't want to cause a panic. Maybe just Mitch and a few men he trusted could cover most of the village.

Landon took another step, listening for any noise that might be human and hoping his eyes would adjust to the darkness so he could see better.

A creaking and squeaking sound alerted Landon. He turned toward where he thought the noise had come from. It might have been a gust of wind pushing on metal. He was aware of his own breathing and his heart drumming in his ear. He took another very cautious step. Now he was only a few feet from the first shed. Up ahead were dozens of possibilities for hiding places.

The hitman didn't have lots of options as it got colder. Would he return to the plane and try to keep warm in there? They still weren't sure where the pilot had gone. What if he was somehow connected to the hitman and helping him?

An awful thought entered his mind. What if the two of them held one of the villagers hostage, so they would have a warm place to stay through the night? He couldn't let that happen.

Doing the search alone was not a good idea. At the very least, he needed to enlist Mitch's help. There was no official permanent law here in the village, but Mitch probably knew men he could depend on when any crime occurred.

Landon turned slightly, preparing to head back to Mitch's trailer as a plan formed in his mind. They'd have to post a guard by the plane to make sure the two men didn't return to it. Even if they couldn't leave until the fog lifted, they might try to hide there.

A scuffing noise caused him to pivot. A weight like

a wall slammed into him and knocked him on his back. He'd lost his grip on the gun in the fall.

The attacker pummeled him in the face. Landon recovered enough to land a jab to the man's stomach before the guy got in several more blows. A fist slammed against Landon's neck, taking his breath away. This was the same guy who had attacked him at his house. He used the same tactics.

Landon heard footsteps.

As he struggled to take in air, the man leaped to his feet and all but vaporized. From the other direction, Landon saw a bobbing light—someone was coming toward him. That must be what had scared the attacker away. He heard approaching footsteps and then Natasha was kneeling over him.

"Are you okay?"

He couldn't speak.

Mitch's face came into view as he aimed a flashlight at Landon. "Natasha waited until I got back to come find you."

Mitch's presence must be why the hired gun had run. Otherwise he would have just gone after Natasha.

"I was worried about you," she said. "I know you told me to stay at the trailer."

For once, Landon was glad she hadn't listened to him. Finally, he was able to speak. "He's out there somewhere. We need to find him before he decides to attack one of the villagers to get shelter. Did you see which way he went?"

"No, I just saw you lying on the ground. The guy is gone." Mitch rose from his kneeling position and held a hand out to his friend. "There are a couple of empty houses, he might seek shelter there."

Natasha rose, as well. "You have some cuts on your face."

"I don't want to frighten the whole village, but we need a few men to do a search." Landon felt a little light-headed from the blows he'd received.

Mitch patted his shoulder. "Let's get you some first aid, and we'll come up with a plan. I can send a man to search the plane right away."

As the adrenaline in his system subsided, Landon became aware of the pain from the cuts and bruises on his face. He tasted blood in his mouth. "My gun. I need to find my gun."

Natasha shone the flashlight all around the area where Landon had been knocked down until they retrieved the gun.

They walked back to the trailer. Now more lights were on in more houses. Mitch stood outside the trailer. "I'm going to see what I can put in place with a little help. There's a first-aid kit in the drawer by the sink." Mitch turned and took off at a jog.

Natasha stepped into the trailer. "Let's get you fixed up." She walked over to the drawer and retrieved the first-aid kit, which she placed on the counter. "Mitch threw the breaker when he came in. So we have lights and electricity again."

After locking the door, Landon collapsed on the couch. As long as those two men were out there, they were vulnerable. They still didn't know if the pilot was involved or not.

Seeing how much Landon was bleeding, Natasha opened several cupboards until she found a washcloth, which she ran under the faucet after she let the water warm. She sat beside him and dabbed at the cut on his forehead.

"I suppose I look really pretty right now, huh?"

"Like you went ten rounds with a prizefighter." She pulled the washcloth away. "You have a bruise under your eye." Without thinking, she reached up and touched just outside the area that was growing purple.

His eyes met hers. She remembered the moment they'd shared during the Christmas program, the feathery touch of his fingers on hers. Her mouth parted slightly as she fell into the depth of his brown eyes. He leaned forward and kissed her. His lips brushed gently over hers. Her hand rested on his neck.

Still reeling from the intensity of his touch and closeness, she pulled back. Sadness washed over her. "The kiss that can go nowhere, right?"

"Right." He kept his face close to hers. "I was out of line, sorry."

"It was both our faults." She tried to make her voice sound cold and business-like while butterflies danced in her head and stomach. "Don't form attachments. That's the number one rule." She stared at the floor and then retrieved a bandage from the first-aid kit.

"Sometimes attachments happen whether you want them to or not."

She tore open the bandage wrapper. "I'd be lying if I said I wasn't growing to care for you, Landon, but your life is in Little Bear." She pressed the bandage against his forehead. "Mine will be somewhere else. Who knows where?" She caught the note of bitterness in her voice. She was alive despite the threat against her, but for the last year she had not really been living.

In the brief moment they'd shared the kiss, she'd

felt like she was taking her first breath after being deprived of air.

"I know it's an impossible situation. But let's not lie about how we feel."

She nodded and closed the first-aid kit.

The door swung open and Mitch put his head in. "I got three guys searching the area around the village and the empty houses." He stepped inside. "The way I see it, you guys have two choices. You can stay here until that fog lifts, which should be within the next day or so. Or, option two, we have a villager who needs a dogsled team delivered to a neighboring village. The musher is injured and can't make the delivery herself. You'd be able to catch either a plane or car out of there to wherever you need to go. You could leave within the hour."

Landon glanced over at Natasha. "I don't like putting the whole village at risk."

"I'm fine with the dogsled. If we stay, it's just a matter of time before he comes after me again."

"Maybe you won't have to make that choice," Mitch said. "One of my guys might find him."

"Actually, we think the guy's pilot might be involved. Why else would he be laying low, too?"

"Speaking of pilots. Where is ours at?" Landon asked. "We have to let Ted know what is going on."

"He's probably staying at the red house at the end of the street. The owner of the house runs a sort of informal hotel since her kids moved out. I can let him know what happened with you guys," Mitch said.

"Wait, like, till three hours after we leave and then tell the talkers in the village that we have gone in the opposite direction that we actually went. That should lure the hitman away from the village but keep us safe," Landon said as he rose.

Mitch nodded. "Sure wish our visit could've been a little longer." He stepped forward and gave his friend a bear hug.

"Me, too, brother," Landon said.

The interaction between the two men touched Natasha deeply. Landon was a man with deep attachments, not only in Little Bear. Natasha stood.

Mitch stepped back. "The lady with the dogs is in the Airstream about a block south of the school. Her name is Rachel."

They grabbed the few things they would need, though they'd not even had a chance to unpack. Landon placed his gun in his holster and stepped out first. Natasha waited at the door while he scanned the roof. "I didn't think he'd try the same thing twice, but it pays to be cautious." He held his hand out for her. "Let's get going."

There were still a few people walking around and some of the houses were lit up, loud music playing and laughter spilling out. The celebrations were still going on for some people.

"Let's hurry. The most likely place for him to be watching for us would be around Mitch's place," Landon said.

She knew there was a danger that they would be followed to where they needed to pick up the dog-sled team. She kept pace with Landon. As he walked briskly, it was clear he was on high alert. His gaze never fixed on one spot and he chose a path that kept them in the shadows.

They arrived at the Airstream and were greeted by

a band of barking dogs in their kennels. There was a second building beside the polished aluminum trailer, smoke rising from its chimney. It was, she presumed, where the dogs stayed when it got really cold.

Natasha's mind was still on the kiss she and Landon had shared.

The barking of the dogs fed her fear and jerked her back to reality. She prayed that she and Landon would get out of town safely.

FIFTEEN

Landon stepped forward and knocked on the door of the Airstream. At the sound of the pounding, another set of dogs barked from somewhere unseen. A woman, walking with a limp, came around the side of the trailer.

"You must be Mitch's friends."

"Yes." Landon held out his hand for her to shake. She was an older woman. Her skin was leathery from being out in the elements, but her features were filled with life. "I'm Landon."

"I got the dogs harnessed and ready to go. You two are a blessing. I was going to deliver this team myself and then I went and twisted my ankle." She led them around to the backside of the trailer where the dog team and the sled were waiting.

Landon checked the GPS on his phone.

"It's a straight shot due north to get to the next village," Rachel said. "As long as the weather holds, you should be there by morning. You have some mushing experience, I assume?"

"A little," Landon said.

Landon gestured for Natasha to settle in on the sled.

Rachel retrieved the goggles that were resting on the sled and handed them to Landon. She patted Natasha's shoulder. "I got another pair inside for you. Wait here."

The dogs continued to yip and jump, sensing the excitement of being able to run. "You doing okay?" he asked.

"I'm cozy down here," she said. "You're the one who will feel the bite of the wind."

Landon peered out at the flat landscape beyond the village. "It's pretty calm right now."

Rachel returned with the second set of goggles. And a small box. "Some nourishment for the two of you. The food for the dogs is already packed. They will need to be fed and rested midway."

"Okay," Landon said.

"Once you are over that hill, you should be able to see the lights of the village."

Landon nodded and commanded the dogs to go. The sled jerked forward. Within minutes, they were out in the open beyond Pirta Bay. As the sled glided over the smooth landscape, the dogs pounded out a rhythm. Landon found himself relaxing. The trail was easy enough to follow, and the dogs seemed to know the way. The hours flowed by as they made their way cross country.

The flat terrain transitioned to gradual hills. The dogs slowed from the effort. Off to the side, in the distance, he saw a moose making its way across the white landscape.

They came to the top of the snowy hill. As promised, he could see the twinkling lights of the village far in the distance. He tapped the claw brake with his foot and the dogs stuttered to a halt.

"Might as well rest up the dogs and get some nourishment in them," Landon said.

"I'll help you." Natasha got off the sled, pulled out the phone she'd picked up at Wilhelm's Market and shone the light on the supplies on the sled. She then handed him a bag.

There were six dogs. She continued to root through what had been packed on the sled, retrieving six bowls. After setting out the bowls, Landon portioned the food. The dogs continued to yip and yelp until he unhooked them, and each went to a bowl and ate greedily.

Natasha sat on the edge of the sled and flipped open the box Rachel had given them. "Looks like jerky and candy bars."

"Protein and carbs." Landon sat beside her. "Probably about the same thing the dogs are eating, only in a different form." The food filled him up.

After eating, the dogs settled down and rested. When Landon and Natasha finished their food, he stood. They'd been sitting, facing the direction of where they were going. He looked back to where they had come from down the hill.

He saw two faint lights in the distance. One was moving east to west and the other was heading straight for them on the trail. He tensed. The slowness of the light suggested that what was coming toward them was a dogsled not a snowmobile. People sometimes took their dogs out for night runs.

Natasha came to stand beside him. "Do you think that is someone from the village?"

"Who else could it be?" he said. "Far as I know, there is no one living outside the village in a cabin off by itself. That would just be too dangerous."

He turned his attention to the light that was moving east. It had swung in a semicircle and was now headed more north, toward them. Though it was hard to judge, the speed at which the light moved suggested it might be someone on a snowmobile. "There's not much to do for recreation. People take their dogs and snowmobiles out all the time."

"Sure," Natasha said. "Kind of late for that, though."

Neither one of the them dared say what they were both thinking: that one of those moving lights might indicate they were being tracked.

They hooked the dogs back up to the sled and picked up the now empty bowls. Without a word, Natasha settled into the cargo bed and Landon mushed the dogs into a run again.

The lights of the village loomed in the distance. The dogs running in unison beat out a steady rhythm. Landon peered over his shoulder. Now there were three sets of lights. Two of them seemed to be moving in swirling patterns and the other was heading straight for them.

He thought about trying to reach Mitch via phone or text to see if a snowmobile or dogsled had been stolen, but he doubted there'd be a signal until they got closer to their destination.

He mushed the dogs to go faster and prayed that the lights behind him were just people from the village out to have some nighttime fun.

As they drew closer to their destination, Natasha was unable to let go of the worry that the hitman was once again on their trail. She couldn't see behind her whether or not the lights were still coming toward them. If she angled her body to look, the sled might be thrown off balance. Her view was of what lay ahead. She was grateful for the warm covering. Her feet and fingers were toasty. Only her face was affected by the cold.

It was still dark as they sped by the first house on the outskirts of the village. Though the sky had gone from black to gray, it would be another two or three hours before sunrise. A plume of smoke rose up from the chimney of the house. Though they were still about half a mile away, she had a clear view of the town as they headed downhill. It had actual streets and was built on a grid as opposed to the randomness of Pirta Bay, the village where Mitch lived.

The sweeping, swooshing sound of the sled runners gliding over the snow enveloped her as the dogs' paws, moving in unison, ate up the snow.

A distance boom and a zinging sound destroyed her peace. Her heart raced as terror spread through her.

The hitman's bullet had found them.

She was pretty sure the bullet was embedded in the pile of supplies on the sled. One runner of the sled came off the ground as Landon made a sharp turn, trying to avoid another bullet hitting them.

She looked up in the direction of where the shot had probably come from. The hitman had taken up an off-to-the-side position on the rim of the hill they had just come down. He must be using a rifle to make such a long shot. He had to have been on a snowmobile to get ahead of them.

The only cover was a cluster of trees on the outskirts of town and the house they had passed a few minutes ago. She doubted Landon wanted to put the residents of the house in jeopardy.

Landon mushed the dogs to go faster, steering the sled so they were not moving in a straight line. Her heart raced, and she feared that the hitman would try to stop them by shooting the lead dog.

Another shot rang through the air. This one missed its target. They drew closer to the trees. The sled hit several bumps, which jarred her body and made her bite her tongue.

Once they were in the shelter of the trees, Landon jumped off and made sure the dogs were settled in the thick of the foliage, where they would not be an easy target. Natasha slipped off, as well, using the sled as cover.

There was still not much light to see by. The flash of the rifle as it released a third shot gave away the hitman's location. Both of them crouched behind the sled as the shot reverberated across the barren landscape. They'd veered far enough away to make an accurate shot with a rifle hard.

The dogs were clearly agitated, yipping and pulling on the immobilized sled. Natasha knew they all couldn't stay there for long. Her guess: the assassin would move in, take up a closer position and fire another shot the second they put their heads above the cover of the sled. The trees only partially protected them.

To be fully concealed, she lay on her stomach, facing Landon, who had taken up a similar position. She leaned toward him. Her face was only inches from his. "What are we going to do?"

He craned his neck to look through the other side

of the trees. "He's going to be making his way toward us. We have to get out of here."

"Going back on the road that leads to town would make us easy targets."

He pointed through the trees. "Exactly, so we're not going that way."

Though she could not see much beyond the trees, she suspected that getting off the road meant dealing with rough terrain.

"We might have to lead the dogs." He pointed to the ridge where the rifleman was probably concealed. "Unless he's dressed in all white, we'll see him as he works his way down. There are not that many places to hide."

"He must have driven up there on a snowmobile. No way could he have gotten ahead of us on a dogsled," she said. "What if he just decides to swoop down on the snowmobile?"

"He still has to stop and line up a shot, and we will see him coming. There are a lot of obstacles between us and him if we go on the other side of these trees."

There was also a chance of wrecking, and they would have to move slower. Still, she knew it was the best option where there were no good choices. "I'll run beside the sled so I can duck down and use it for cover if I have to."

"Good. I'm going to get in front in case I have to reroute the dogs so they don't get hit." He squeezed her shoulder. "It's not that far to town. It will be much harder for him to get at us without being caught himself once we make it there."

Fear caused the butterflies in Natasha's stomach again as Landon got in front of the lead dog, grabbed the harness and guided him. She switched off the light positioned on the back of the sled that had helped Landon see the road.

The dogs at first seemed confused. There were fallen logs and snow bumps to navigate over and around. Several times, Natasha grabbed the sled so it wouldn't topple.

A sideways glance revealed only a limited picture of the ridge and the hill leading down toward them. She tensed when she thought she heard the sound of a snowmobile. The sound died out quickly.

The trees grew farther apart. She could see the lights of the village once again. The makeshift path led them in a wide arc. They had only to cross several hundred yards out in the open before they would be at the edge of town and protected by the shelter of the buildings.

Landon brought the dogs to a halt while they were still hidden in the trees. "This will be the most dangerous part. It looks pretty smooth. I say we get on and make a run for it."

Natasha felt her blood run cold as she stared out at the stretch of flat land that led to the village. The hitman would probably be waiting for them to emerge from the shelter of the trees. She reached out and petted the husky closest to the sled. Landon stroked the head of the lead dog. They were risking the safety of the dogs, as well. "What if we left them behind and came back for them with something we could load them into?"

"It bothers me, too," Landon said. "I don't think we could run fast enough to avoid being hit. We have a chance on the sled."

She knew he was right. Even if they made it, she wasn't sure if she could forgive herself if something happened to even one of the dogs. She got onboard. Landon's voice sounded behind her as he mounted up, as well. "Stay as low as you can."

"I know."

He eased forward, going slow at first through the last of the trees.

Natasha kept her eyes on the path into town. And then she looked up at the hill where the shooter was probably hiding behind a rock or a snowdrift. There were a few dark spots on the landscape, which could be rocks or brush, but nothing moved. Still, they had to assume they were still in the hitman's sights.

Landon commanded the dogs to go faster. They sped up, racing out into the open. Natasha crouched low in the sled and braced for a bullet to come at them.

SIXTEEN

Aware of how exposed they were for the next few minutes, Landon opted to move as fast as possible while steering the sled in an erratic curving pattern to make them harder to hit.

The dogs seemed to increase their speed as they got closer to the outskirts of town. Landon heard the boom of a shot being fired and crouched, still trying to keep control of the sled. His heart raced. The dogs stuttered and slowed. He feared the worst, but they recovered quickly and pushed the final stretch toward a cabin with a sign out front that said Last Stop Café.

As they entered the city limits, Landon glanced at the hill from where the shots had been fired. He saw a dark spot moving up the hill. The shooter was probably going back to where he'd parked the snowmobile. Landon speculated that he would come into town to try to get at Natasha.

They passed another business with a truck and several snowmobiles parked outside. Once the shooter came into town, he'd be impossible to tell from anyone else. Though he knew the build of the hitman, Landon had never really gotten a good look at his face.

They had to get out of this village as quickly as possible. Mitch had said the roads were passable by car, but that a plane would be faster. The town's main street was about five blocks in length with mostly residential houses on either side. He checked his GPS for the location of where they were supposed to deliver the dogs. When they arrived at the house, he could see the landing strip on the outskirts of town. Several planes were parked there. They needed to find out when the next plane was leaving.

There was a truck parked outside the house and Landon noticed there were three windows on either side of the enclosed truck bed. Each window probably fronted an individual crate for a sled dog.

An older man stared at them through the window of the house and then came out to greet them. "You made it." He bent over to pet the lead dog and then he touched each dog on the head.

"They did really good. Amazing animals." Landon felt his heart swell with gratitude for the dogs and that they had all made it unscathed.

"That, they are," the old man said. "You folks can come in for some hot tea if you like. Wife made some blueberry muffins."

"I wish we could." Natasha had gotten off the sled and now stood beside Landon.

"Do you know when the next plane leaves here?"

The old man straightened. "This isn't LAX, son. They're not on a schedule. The pilots tend to hang out at the Last Stop Café until they have enough passengers to justify flying out or a passenger willing to pay enough to make the run worth their while."

Landon shook his head. "Of course that's how it works."

The old man pointed to one of the two planes. "That guy brings in supplies and people pretty regular. I think he's waiting on some hunters he needs to transport."

"What is his name?"

"LeRoy O'Conner. Usually wears a bomber jacket and blue scarf."

Natasha and Landon said goodbye to the dogs and headed back toward the main street. When they were about a block away, Landon turned and continued walking through the residential area. "I think we're more of a target on Main Street. Let's take the back way to the café."

Though there were not many people outside, lights glowed from the houses. They even saw the occasional glow of a television set.

"I hope we can get out of here fast," Natasha said.

"Me, too." As they got closer to the café, he saw trailers behind it that probably served as hotel rooms.

Natasha kept pace with him as they walked along the side of the Last Stop Café. There were two more snowmobiles parked out front than there had been when they'd entered town. As he opened the door to the café, Landon was aware that the hitman might already be the cafe.

A momentary hush settled around them as they entered. All eyes were on them and then normal activity resumed. There were four men in the corner, playing cards, and two sitting at the bar, eating. Two other people sat at tables by themselves. One man had his back to the room, only a cup of coffee on his table. The other, a teenager reading a book, took the occasional bite from a stack of pancakes. The only woman in the place was the cook who was frying bacon and sausage on the grill.

Landon didn't see anyone matching the description of the man who was the most likely candidate for flying them out of there.

The cook, who must also be the only waitress, left her grill after loading up a couple of plates. She took them to the men playing cards, wiped her hands on her apron and then looked at Landon and Natasha. "What can I get you folks?"

"We're looking for a man named LeRoy O'Conner."

"I think he went to get some shut-eye." She turned slightly to look at the clock mounted in the kitchen. "He'll probably be up in a bit, if you want to wait around for him. I know he is hoping to take off today. I can get you folks something to eat while you wait."

Landon wasn't crazy about staying out in the open like this. Though the man after Natasha was unlikely to come in a take her out with witnesses, it seemed like either moving around or staying hidden would be the better choice.

Natasha squeezed his biceps. "We can't afford to miss LeRoy and have him take off without us."

Landon glanced around again. He was hungry. The food they'd eaten midway through their journey had been used up. He picked a table that was not by a window and more in the corner of the room, by the restroom. He chose the chair that gave him a constant view of the café and the door. Natasha settled into the chair beside his.

The man with his back to the room had turned slightly when they'd entered but had not looked directly at them. His behavior was a bit off-putting. It was possible that he was just antisocial. Plenty of people that lived in these remote places could be that way. Still, it was as if he didn't want people to see his face.

Landon had not seen the hitman's face, and this guy had a different build. A thought rushed through his head. He also had not gotten a good look at the plane that had brought the assassin into Mitch's village. It was possible, then, that the second plane out on the runway might belong to the shooter's pilot. Landon had no idea when or if the fog had lifted, but it wouldn't have been a long flight to get here. There had also been significant cloud cover, so it was possible they could have missed the plane or it had taken a route that hadn't passed over them. So, while the hitman had been trailing them on a snowmobile, the pilot could be waiting in this town.

The waitress/cook brought them each a menu. "Lot of the stuff is canned, sorry about that. I do try to be creative, but the eggs are fresh, not powdered."

"Thank you." Landon glanced down at the menu.

The woman walked away.

Natasha leaned close to whisper in Landon's ear. "That guy in the corner of the room with his back to us makes me nervous. The way he's acting is a little weird. Who doesn't at least make eye contact with other people when they enter a room? Everyone else stared at us for five seconds."

"Me, too," Landon said. "Do you think he might be the pilot who transported the hitman?"

Natasha shook her head and spoke under her breath. "Could be. We never saw the guy." She drew her attention to the menu. "What looks good to you?"

"I think you can't go wrong with bacon and eggs and pancakes." He cut his gaze again toward the man sitting with his back to everyone.

"The cook should bring that out pretty fast. We need to be ready to go if LeRoy shows up."

A roar of laughter came from the table where the four men were playing cards. The sudden noise made Landon tense.

Natasha placed her palm on her chest and leaned a little closer to Landon. "That about gave me a heart attack, too."

The waitress/cook came and took their order.

"I just hope this LeRoy guy shows up like the waitress said he would," Natasha said.

"If he's not here by the time we finish eating, I say we knock on his door and wake him. I know it's rude and we won't exactly be getting off on the right foot."

As the woman set two glasses of orange juice in front of them, Landon tilted his head and asked, "Do you know that man sitting over there by himself, not looking at anyone."

The waitress/cook straightened. "Yeah. He lives just up the street. Comes every day. I've gotten a couple of words out of him. My guess is PTSD issues. It's probably a challenge for him to even come here. Bless the poor man."

The woman walked away.

"So that blows that theory," Landon said, pulling his phone out. He had a signal. "I'm going to call Mitch. We know what happened to the hitman, but we still don't know about the pilot." Landon pressed his friend's number.

Mitch picked up on the second ring. "Hey, you guys made it?"

"Sort of. We still have to get a flight out. We were followed. Is anyone missing a snowmobile?"

"Yes, actually," Mitch said.

"And what about the pilot? Is he still there?"

"He took off as soon as the fog lifted. He must have been watching the plane, waiting for his chance when we didn't have someone patrolling the dock."

So one of the planes on the tarmac could belong to the hitman's pilot.

Landon looked up as the waitress/cook carried two plates toward their table. "Don't want to take up too much of your time. Wish our visit could have been longer."

"Next time, my friend," Mitch said.

"Thanks for your help."

The woman set the plates down in front of them and walked away. After explaining to Natasha about the pilot, Landon dug into his eggs and munched on his bacon, still watching the room. Though the food was satisfying, his need to remain on high alert and the tension it created in his stomach meant that he really didn't enjoy the flavors as much as he could have.

Two more men who did not match the description of the pilot, LeRoy O'Connor, came in and sat at the bar. Judging by the way they were dressed, they were probably snowmobilers, though it appeared they had walked here. The same number of snowmobiles was still outside.

Landon had scraped the last of his eggs off the plate and taken the final sip of orange juice when the door opened and a man wearing a bomber jacket and blue scarf stepped in.

Both of them rose. While Landon pulled his wallet out and put a twenty on the table, Natasha scooted her chair back and walked over to the man they presumed was LeRoy O'Conner.

Landon listened to Natasha's hushed voice explain their situation as LeRoy walked toward them.

"I got room for three more," LeRoy said. "If you'll help me load the cargo, I'll take some off of the price of your fare. We'll take off as soon as I get something to eat. In about twenty minutes, be at the plane, ready to go."

More waiting, Landon thought. "Where exactly are you set to land?"

"Got a stop at Wasilla and then on to Anchorage," LeRoy told them.

"We'd like to go all the way to Anchorage," Landon said.

After LeRoy walked up to the counter to put in a food order, Landon looked around to see if there was a rear exit door they could use but didn't see one. It was probably off a back room via the kitchen. As they stepped outside through the front door, he was aware of all the places a man could hide with a rifle. The building across the street was two stories high. There was an incline where trees could hide a man behind the street.

Landon ushered Natasha back toward the residential houses.

"Twenty minutes feels like an eternity," she said.

"I don't want to be sitting out there on the tarmac. We might as well put a Shoot Me sign around our necks."

"Guess we just walk slow," she said. "And try not to call attention to ourselves."

Despite the chill, they were both dressed in clothes that kept them warm.

They walked past a house where five children played in the yard making snow angels and building a snowman. A woman holding a coffee cup stood on the porch, watching them. As the late-in-the-day sun came up, the little town seemed to be waking, too.

Landon wove through the neighborhood that only extended three blocks. They walked, their boots clumping on the snow-packed ground that served as a sidewalk. He found himself wanting to hold Natasha's hand but realized that such a gesture would be wrong. The kiss, however wonderful, had been out of line. They both knew that.

They passed a house where the owner had gone all out with the Christmas decorations, which still had a warm glow in the morning light. Was it really December 24? Ever since all of this had started with Natasha, his life had taken on a surreal quality. Though work as a trooper did have exciting moments, he felt like he'd been pulled from his dull life into something much more engaging. Knowing that his one job right now was to protect Natasha until she could step into her new life gave him a renewed sense of purpose.

The one thing that had changed for the good was that the numbness he'd felt since Maggie's death seemed to have lifted. Was it the threat of death that made him feel so alive or being close to Natasha?

They came to the final house on the street, which opened up to the tarmac and runway. No one was around. Landon shrank back, looking for a hiding place that would provide them a view of the tarmac so they would know when LeRoy and his other passengers showed up.

"Over there." Natasha pointed to a little shack on the edge of the tarmac that may have at one time been a coffee take-out hut but now looked abandoned.

They walked the short distance to it. The door was unlocked.

"This looks like it's the airport waiting room and a defunct coffee hut," Landon said.

They stepped inside. There were three battered folding chairs. They took their seats, which gave them a view of the tarmac through the drive-through order window. Shortly after they sat, a truck pulled up beside one of the airplanes. The bed of the truck was covered in a tarp.

"That must be the cargo LeRoy referenced," Natasha said.

The driver turned off the truck and waited in the cab. A few minutes later, three people emerged from the direction of Main Street and came to stand by the airplane and truck.

Landon scanned the area all around the tarmac. There were several trucks at the far end that he guessed were used for refueling the planes. Other than that, the area was open. "I wonder what's keeping LeRoy."

"Remember what the old dog musher said. This isn't LAX. I think LeRoy shows up when he is good and ready." She laughed a little. "You have to admit. That was a funny thing to say. You being an Alaska native should know how things run in these remote locations."

He laughed, too. And shook his head. "So, it was

a little presumptuous of me to think things run on a schedule."

She leaned against him, so their shoulders were touching. Even through the thickness of their winter clothes, her being so close brought back the memory of the kiss they'd shared.

Movement in his peripheral vision caught his eye. He turned his head. His heart skipped up a notch until he saw that it was LeRoy emerging from one of the side streets and headed straight toward the plane.

"Guess we better get out there and earn our keep," Landon said.

They stood and stepped out onto the snow-covered tarmac. The truck driver had jumped out and pulled back the tarp on the truck bed. The cargo, mostly wooden statues carved with a chainsaw, also included some smaller wrapped packages. LeRoy opened the cargo bay underneath the plane. It looked to Landon like some light building materials were already taking up some of the space. Materials, most likely, for delivery to some other small, isolated town.

Once the cargo was loaded, the five passengers got on board. LeRoy was already sitting in front of his instrument panel looking at a document on a clipboard. "Pick a seat, any seat," he said.

Landon settled in a window seat at the back of the plane. Natasha sat beside him. The other three men settled in, as well. After he collected everyone's fair, LeRoy fired up his plane, closed the entry door and took his seat in the cockpit.

There was a knock on the door.

With a groan, LeRoy got out of his seat and opened the door. Though they could not see who he was talking to from their side of the plane at the back and opposite the door, the conversation sounded friendly enough. LeRoy exited the plane. The cargo bay was opened once again and something was put inside.

A moment later, LeRoy stepped back in, putting some cash in his pocket. He smiled at the passengers. "Looks like we'll be traveling with a full load folks."

A man got on the plane taking the empty seat right behind the pilot. The seat backs were high and Landon couldn't see the man's face but the final passenger had the same build as the hitman.

SEVENTEEN

Natasha noticed that the Landon tensed when the last-minute passenger showed up and took a seat. She leaned close and whispered in his ear, "Do you think it's him?"

Landon kept his eyes on the mysterious passenger though the view was only of his arm and the top of his head. "I never got a good look at him, but that guy has the same build as our hitman. They loaded something into the cargo bay before he got on. It could be his rifle."

As LeRoy taxied across the tarmac and positioned the plane at the end of the runway, Natasha gripped the armrests. The butterflies in her stomach were acting up again.

Landon put his hand on top of hers. "For someone who doesn't like to fly, you sure are doing a lot of it."

His hand felt warm and his touch calmed her somewhat. She appreciated his sensitivity about her feelings. "Maybe as soon as we level off, you can move up and see if you can get a look at him."

"Good idea. I never really saw his face, but his reaction will tell me everything," Landon said. "It seems like a bold move to me to get on the plane with us."

"If that other plane wasn't his pilot's, maybe this was the only way he could not lose us," she said.

"He's not likely to try anything with all these people around…if it is him."

LeRoy pushed the plane forward, gaining speed and then lifting off. The butterflies coalesced into a tight ball in her stomach. The ascent when the plane was at an angle was the worst part for her. Landon kept his hand on hers.

She closed her eyes and took several deep breaths. The plane leveled off.

LeRoy spoke up. "Folks, I need you to stay in your seats. Looks like we're going to hit some turbulence right away."

"Oh great—" Before Natasha could complete her sentence, the plane bumped up and down. Her seat belt pressed into her skin. She felt nauseous.

"It's worse in the small planes. You feel everything." Landon's voice was gentle, filled with compassion.

After about ten minutes, the turbulence became less jarring. Landon unclicked his seat belt. "I'm going to pretend like I want to have conversation with the pilot. See how our mystery passenger reacts to me."

A clanging noise caused the plane to jerk. The engine sounded like it had sputtered, or maybe it was something else. Everyone on the plane visibly tensed. The passengers who had been chatting fell silent. LeRoy stared at his instrument panel. His shoulders nearly touched his ears.

Something was wrong.

"Folks, I think we will have to turn around. There is something going on with one of my engines. I just can't take a chance," LeRoy said.

Natasha pressed her head back against the seat, fighting off the despair she felt. Tears warmed her eyes. When was this going to be over?

Landon grabbed her hand and pressed it between both of his. She turned to gaze into his brown eyes. The anguish she felt wasn't just about the delay in meeting up with Marshal Henderson. She knew that once she did, she'd have to say goodbye to Landon.

"Thank you for seeing me through all of this," she said.

"I wouldn't have it any other way," he said.

The plane seemed to be losing and then gaining altitude as it limped back to the tarmac. LeRoy talked in a low voice on the radio. He probably didn't want to worry his passengers, but it was clear from his tone that they were in an emergency situation.

When she glanced through Landon's window, all she saw was trees. They must be getting close. The plane lost altitude and then suddenly they were bumping along the runway. Her body was jerked one way and then the other. Landon never let go of her hand.

The plane came to a sudden stop.

LeRoy jumped up from his seat and opened the exit door. He turned to face the passengers. "Please exit in an orderly fashion front to back." His attempt to sound calm was thwarted by the waver in his voice.

The mystery passenger got up first and disappeared.

Natasha had only a glimpse of him from the side. Long hair had hung in his face.

The passengers exited. Before the last one was down the four stairs that led to the tarmac, she had released her seat belt and stood. Landon was right behind her. Even before her feet touched the snowy ground, she heard a fire engine as it rolled toward the plane. Something must be on fire. LeRoy got out of the plane and hurried around the back of the plane.

Natasha noted that the other plane that had been on the tarmac earlier was gone. She could feel her mood sinking. How were they going to get out of here?

All the passengers but the mystery passenger stood some distance away, watching as the fire truck disappeared on the other side of the plane. LeRoy came around to their side of the plane. "You folks all okay?"

Everyone nodded.

"Guess we're spending Christmas here," one of the passengers said.

Landon wrapped an arm around her back and squeezed her shoulder. "I'll show my trooper credentials and commandeer us a car. We'll drive through the night."

"We're missing someone." LeRoy turned one way and then the other. "Did anyone see where that last passenger went?"

Everyone shook their heads.

Natasha studied the belly of the plane where the cargo bay at been left open. She stepped toward LeRoy and spoke under her breath. "Looks like he grabbed his baggage before he disappeared. Do you know what he stashed under there?"

LeRoy shook his head. "Whatever it was, it was wrapped in a blanket. Sort of long and narrow. Part of my job is not to ask questions."

A chill ran down her spine. So it could have been a rifle. She studied the trees that surrounded the tarmac. Was he hiding out there, waiting to take his shot?

Landon grabbed her arm. "Let's see if we can get a vehicle. Towns like this don't have a lot of law enforcement but they usually have a mayor or something."

The other passengers drifted away after LeRoy refunded their money. Landon approached LeRoy, who handed him the cash he had paid. "Do you know someone who might be headed toward Anchorage today?"

"On Christmas Eve? Most people are with their families, eating too much and watching Christmas movies."

"Do you know someone who could loan us a vehicle? Is there a mayor in this town?"

"The mayor is also the fire chief, so he's on the other side of the plane."

She glanced again toward the trees and grabbed Landon's arm. "I would feel better if we weren't out in the open like this."

"I agree," he said.

They hurried around to the other side of the plane where a fireman was winding up a hose. The fire engine looked like it was from the seventies.

Landon pulled his badge out from where he kept it in his chest pocket. "I need to transport this woman to Anchorage ASAP. We were hoping to fly out. Is there anyone headed that way or maybe there is a vehicle we could borrow?"

The man who had white hair and a beard looked at them for long moment after studying Landon's badge.

"Please, sir, it's quite serious. This woman is in danger."

"I suppose I can find you something. I have a brother in Anchorage. We'll make arrangements for him to come get the car." He pointed to the fire truck. "Get in."

Natasha breathed a sigh of relief once she was inside the cab of the fire truck.

Within the hour, the mayor/fire chief having found them an older car with a full tank of gas, they were on their way.

The road they drove on was often only one lane. After two hours, they had seen only one other car. Sparkling lights in the distance suggested small settlements or maybe even a farm with several buildings.

They had agreed to switch off driving with her going first. Landon crawled into the back of the car to sleep. With the headlights illuminating for only a short distance, the road clipped by. She felt a little fatigued herself. She wished she had a radio station or book on tape to keep her awake.

She looked ahead at the long, straight stretch of road. When she checked her rearview mirror, her breath caught. Behind her, she saw the glow of two headlights.

She was pretty sure they were being followed.

Natasha's voice seemed to come from very far away as she said his name softly several times.

Landon opened his eyes. "Yes," he said.

"I don't want to alarm you, but there's a car behind us. What are the chances of someone else being on this road on Christmas Eve?"

Landon checked his watch. He'd been asleep for several hours. It was getting close to the time when he was supposed to take over the driving. He straightened and looked out the back window at the other car.

"How long has he been there?"

"I noticed him about ten minutes ago. I just went

over a bunch of hills, so maybe he was there earlier."
She glanced again in the mirror. "Now that we're on a
straight part of the road, he keeps getting closer, like
he's trying to close the distance between us."

His body tensed. "Is there anywhere else he could
have come from besides the town we left?"

"Sure, I saw lights in the distance that could have
been little settlements or several buildings. What bothers me is that there are only two of us on this road. For
the most part, there is no way to pass. Why does he
keep getting closer? When I speed up, he speeds up."

Landon leaned over the seat. Natasha was pushing
sixty, which was about as fast as she could go without
risking an accident given how poorly maintained the
road was.

"As soon as you see a place to pull off the road,
we'll switch drivers. There's got to be a gas station
or something somewhere along here." Again, Landon
glanced out the back window at the menacing yellow
headlights. He was even closer than before. "If he goes
by, maybe he was just a guy trying to stay awake by
being a jerk and playing a game with you. People have
been known to do that."

Natasha sped up even more as the car behind them
drew closer. There were no lights anywhere up ahead.
He appreciated how coolheaded she was despite the
fear she must be wrestling with.

They drove for another twenty minutes. A sign on
the road said another town was five miles away. The
other car was now maybe ten feet behind them.

"I can't go any faster. If I hit a patch of ice, we're
toast."

"I agree," he said.

The road turned into a two-lane. She slowed down. Still, the other driver did not pass. They climbed a hill. Landon had a view of the town when they came down the other side. It didn't look like much. A single streetlamp illuminated a building but there were no lights on inside. Of course, nothing was open Christmas Eve. He could see some other lights farther away that might be houses.

He suspected the population of the settlement was less than a hundred. As they drew closer, he saw that the dark building was a grocery store and post office.

"Should I pull in there? What do you think?"

"Sure. It's a paved parking lot and it looks like they plowed recently." He touched his gun where it rested in the holster. "Don't signal before you turn in. That other car doesn't need to have a warning of what our plan is."

She nodded and sped up as though she were going to drive past the building. At the last second, she turned.

The other car shot past them. Landon stared at the red taillights. It didn't look like the car was slowing.

She turned into the lot, leaving their vehicle running while she opened the door and hurried around to the front passenger side. Landon pushed his door open, stepped out and got in behind the wheel. He glanced at the road, seeing only darkness. That didn't mean the guy wasn't looking for a place to turn around and come back at them.

Landon shifted into Reverse, got turned around and headed for the parking lot exit.

Natasha stared through the windshield at the distant houses with their glowing golden windows. Snow had started to drift down in soft swirling patterns and the moon was only partially covered by clouds. "It's so quiet here."

"Silent night, holy night," he said.

"Last Christmas was pretty crazy. I had just testified at Tan Creti's trial. I celebrated with the police officer assigned to watch me at the safe house. They were able to set things up so my sister and my nephew could come by for a couple of hours, but I'd say this Christmas Eve has that one beat."

He picked up on the note of sadness in her voice. "I'm glad I'm here with you anyway."

"For now," she said.

Landon pulled out of the parking lot, wondering if she, too, was thinking that every mile brought them closer to saying goodbye. He studied the main road and the one perpendicular to it. They didn't have much choice but to go back up on the main road.

"Do you think that guy was just someone late in getting to a relative's house or something?"

"I don't know." He was fully aware that the driver could have pulled off somewhere and was preparing to line up a shot at them. "Let's hope that is the case." He clicked off the headlights and slowed down. "All the same, we don't need to make ourselves an easy target."

He stared through the windshield and falling snow, moving his gaze from side to side, looking for possibilities for a hiding place for a sniper. They came to a sign that announced they were exiting the city limits. He continued to drive. Fluffy snow danced and twirled past the windshield.

Natasha yawned and rested her head on the seat

back. "Now I wish I had crawled into the back, like you did, to sleep." She turned her head toward him and closed her eyes. Within minutes, it was clear she was asleep. Despite what might lay ahead, there was something peaceful about seeing her sleep.

Another half hour passed, and she awoke with a start.

"You okay?"

She nodded.

"No bad dreams?"

"I wish I could say no to that question."

"I'm glad you're awake. You can keep me company. I was getting really bored." He pointed at the dashboard. "This car is so old, it has a cassette deck."

She laughed. "I've heard about those. I didn't realize that was what it was."

"Check the glove compartment to see if there are any tapes in there."

She shrugged and opened it up. She pulled out two cassettes. "So, it looks like we have some children's music or eighties' hit-makers."

"Tough choice. You pick."

She laughed and pushed a tape into the deck. The drum track of the first rock song came on.

"I know this one. My dad used to listen to this stuff when he was working in the garage." Landon started to sing along. She joined in. By the third song, they were laughing at their inability to hit high notes or sing on pitch.

His voice faltered when the car began to wobble and swerve. One of their tires had blown. He gripped the steering wheel and slowed down. "Just what we need—a flat tire."

She clicked off the music. "It's not an accident, Landon. I think I saw the flash of a rifle up there. Someone took a shot at the car."

EIGHTEEN

Before she had even completed her sentence, another shot was fired. Judging from the way the car wobbled and jerked, the bullet had gone through the body of the car. Heart racing, she ducked down. The shots were coming from her side of the vehicle.

The car lumbered along as though it had square wheels. Landon gripped the wheel and crouched low in his seat. "We're not going to get much farther in this thing."

"It's still the safest place right now." She lifted her head, trying to see where the shooter might be, staring at where she thought the shot had come from. She saw only shadows falling over the snow-covered hills.

Landon's voice jittered from the vibrations of the car. "You're probably right."

The car jerked and then came to a full stop. The engine was still running. Landon turned it off. They both hunkered down in their seats, so their heads were beneath the dashboard.

The level of terror she felt was like a weight on her chest, making it hard to breathe. "What do we do now?"

"The shots came from your side of the car. He's probably up on that hill. It will take him at least ten to fifteen minutes to reposition and get closer to the road."

"But then he can just come up to the car and pick us off. Even if you're able to get a couple of shots off, you would be guessing. We can't see him in the dark."

"I don't think he wants to get that close unless he's forced to," Landon said. "He must know that I am armed."

"Then you think he'll take up a position and wait for us to put our heads above the dashboard."

Landon shook his head. "There are a lot of what-ifs and maybes going on here. This is what we know. This car is toast, it's not going to get us to Anchorage. There might be one spare tire in the trunk, but we can't change it with a sniper waiting to pick us off."

"So you're saying we should leave the car and take our chances out there in the cold?"

"He came in a car, too. It's got to be parked somewhere. While he works his way down here, assuming that is what he is doing, maybe we can find his car. It's our only hope. If we stay here, this car will be our coffin."

She took in a breath. "Okay, tell me how that is going to work."

"We slip out of my side of the car, so he doesn't see us. I'm assuming he's got a scope on that rifle that functions in the same way as night-vision goggles. Otherwise, he would not have been able to get such an accurate shot off. We slip around to the back of the car and then head up the hill, where he was, to see if we can find his car."

The plan was rife with potential for them to be killed

or freeze in the cold. They were assuming the hitman would change positions and work his way toward their car. They were assuming they would be able to find the guy's vehicle. But it was the only plan that even gave them a fighting chance. "Okay, let's go."

He clicked open his door as little as possible and slipped to the ground. After zipping her coat up and putting her gloves back on, Natasha crawled across the seat. She placed her hands on the ground, angled her body sideways and pulled forward, pressing her body against the car and dragging her legs until her feet touched the ground, as well. Such an acrobatic act meant the door would not be open very wide, so if the shooter had even a partial view of that side of the car, he wouldn't see that they were escaping.

She turned and shut the door as quietly as possible. She crawled down the length of the car. Landon was waiting for her, crouching by the back bumper. She slipped in behind him and he inched toward the edge of the car. The road dropped off into a ditch beyond which was the hill. There was not much to use for cover on their way up. An exposed rock here and there, a clump of snow-covered bushes.

They dipped down into the ditch.

Landon whispered, "Go slow. He'll be looking for movement."

She closed her eyes and said a quick prayer before crawling up the hill an inch at a time. She supposed if the hitman did fire in this direction, it meant he had seen them and figured out their plan. Natasha only hoped the bullet he fired wouldn't be fatal to either her or Landon.

She reached a bush that allowed her to hide and

catch her breath. She turned her head sideways, in the direction of the two shots, but couldn't see anything. Despite her winter gear, a chill sank into her skin.

She turned her head to where Landon lay flat on his stomach, moving at a snail's pace. She exhaled. A horrible realization sank in. It was so cold, the sniper would be able to see their breath.

The zing of a rifle shot broke the silence of the night. The shot had been aimed below her. At Landon.

Dear God, don't let that bullet find its target.

The quiet settled in around Natasha as she struggled to keep her breaths as shallow as possible.

"He knows where we are. We might as well make a run for it. See those trees up ahead?" The sound of Landon's soft voice was like music to her ears. "We both run at the same time. But stay far apart."

"You got it. Let's go."

She burst to her feet and ran. The incline of the hill strained her leg muscles as her boots dug into the snow. She dropped to the ground. She could just make out Landon off to the side as he did the same thing.

Natasha jumped to her feet again and sprinted. The trees loomed in front of her. Though she wasn't crazy about being target practice for a shooter, it bothered her that there were no more rifle shots being fired. That meant he might be moving closer to them.

Landon nearly slammed into her as he made it to the trees, as well.

"We can't stay here. He might be swinging around and getting closer to line up a better shot," he said. "He must be repositioning, otherwise he would have fired a shot."

The cluster of short evergreens was maybe ten feet

wide and five feet deep. The trees were their only viable cover. The hitman had to know that this was where they would run. "Do you suppose he's waiting for us to come out on the uphill side?"

"Probably," Landon said. "So we run in a straight line away from the trees, due south. The trees will shield us. It will take him a minute to figure out what we've done." That meant they probably wouldn't find the guy's car, assuming he had parked it somewhere close to where he was positioned.

She burst from the safety of the evergreens, Landon's footsteps crunching behind her. They were running into the unknown.

They ran for about ten minutes, their boots sinking into the deep snow. Her muscles fatigued, and she was out of breath. Both of them slowed, though it was hard to see much of anything. When she glanced over her shoulder, she saw no moving shadows. All around her was snow-covered hills with only a little vegetation.

Perhaps they had managed to delay the assassin from catching up with them, but they still were not in a good spot. Even with the warm weather gear they wore, they could not stay outside for long without being affected by the cold. It was too far to walk back to the little town with the closed store.

A gust of wind blew snow at her. She walked even slower. The chill bore into her face and she zipped her coat up to the neck. "We have to find some shelter," she said.

"I agree. Let's move up the hill. That will provide us with view of more of our surroundings."

As they worked their way to the ridgeline, she stared back at the way they had come. Their footprints were the only ones in the snow. Once the shooter figured out which direction they had fled, they would be easy to track.

As the cold settled into her bones, so did a sense of hopelessness. They had not avoided death, only delayed it.

Landon knew that it was just a matter of time before they were in the crosshairs of the hitman's rifle again. He needed to come up with some sort of plan to keep them alive. They could continue to step out into the unknown and hope they would find help or shelter, or they could work with what they knew.

"Natasha, let's head down to the road. We are more likely to run into someone down there."

Without a word, she did an about-face and headed back down the hill. There was no way to cover their tracks. When he glanced off to the side, he still saw no sign of the shooter. He knew from experience that the man would not give up.

"I know you're cold. I am, too. But we need to pick up the pace."

Partway down the hill, they came to a grove of trees. They sprinted through them. Darkness and the canopy of branches made it hard to see. A least they weren't contending with the deep snow. Once they were free of the cover of the trees, Landon chose a path that ran parallel to what he thought was the road. If the shooter figured out where they were going, he might just take a shortcut and wait for them there. They didn't want to walk into an ambush.

Every few minutes, either he or Natasha glanced over their shoulders.

"It makes me more nervous when he's not shooting at us."

"Me, too. It makes me wonder if he's come up with different plan." Landon glanced higher up the hill at their backs. It was possible that, with night vision, the man with the rifle would just move to a high spot and wait, assuming that sooner or later he would see them.

They had not seen so much as a deer since they'd left the car. For someone with a keen eye, which this guy had, any motion would be easy enough to spot.

By the time they got to the road, both were moving slower. At least the snow on the road was packed down. They had a choice to make. To move in the direction of the defunct car or to work back toward the little town they'd stopped to switch drivers at and hope they ran into someone.

Natasha stood beside him. "Going back to that little town would take a long time."

He took out his cell phone. No signal. "We have a chance of finding help at the town. And I suspect if there is no cell service, someone will have a landline."

Landon's mind was reeling. It seemed strange that a shot had not been fired at them for so long. Though he kept the thought to himself, he wondered if the shooter had gone back to his car and decided to track them, knowing that eventually they would probably go back to the road.

"I'm tired and cold," she said.

He gathered her into his arms and held her. "I'm tired, too, but we have to keep moving." He directed her off the road to a place where they would still have a view of it as they worked their way through the brush that helped to conceal them.

She walked beside him. The padding of their boots in the snow was the only sound.

"Worst Christmas ever?"

The question surprised him. Maybe talking would keep them both from thinking about how cold they were. "Actually, second worse. I had to do a stakeout one Christmas Eve for a guy that never showed up. The coffee was cold. The doughnuts were rock hard, and I was by myself. At least I'm here with you. That makes it okay."

She turned to face him. "You mean that? Even knowing that he's out there waiting to put a bullet in each of us?"

"Yes, even with that." Landon pulled his glove off and placed his hand on her cheek. She looked up at him. He felt drawn to her, wanted to kiss her again, but then sadness washed over him. There would come a time when they'd have to say goodbye…if they got to Anchorage alive.

"Freeze this moment in your mind because it's precious," she said. "Thank you, Landon, for all that you have done for me. Just want you to know that."

Was she thinking that they weren't going to get out of this alive? He leaned in and kissed her forehead. He pulled back and studied her face. "I don't know what is going to happen, Natasha. We're not in a good situation."

"Kiss me even if it's a goodbye kiss."

She was right. No matter what, they would be saying goodbye. "Goodbye" because if they made it to Anchorage and were able to do the handoff with the marshal, they would never see each other again. Or "goodbye" because they might simply not make it out of this situation alive.

His lips pressed against hers, and time seemed to stand still. Her hand rested against his chest. He pulled back, not wanting the moment to end. Her eyes seemed to be searching his. Then she turned away. "Let's keep going. I'm going to pray while we walk."

"Me, too." He prayed silently for God to show him what to do next. To bring shelter or a plan so they were not out in the cold all night. To find a way to be free of being hunted by the mafia's hired gun.

The cover of the brush ended and they stepped out in the open. Though they were some distance from it, he could still discern the road. When he looked up at the hill they had descended, he saw a tiny light moving in a curving line.

"That has to be him," he said. "It's going to take him at least twenty minutes to get down to the road and a little while to figure which way we went. I say we double back to the car because it's closer than that little town. We fix that tire and we take off."

She nodded. "Let's make a run for it. We can go up to the road for a while. It will be faster."

She took off running at a diagonal toward the road. His feet pounded behind her.

It was the first time since they'd abandoned the car that he felt hope again. The fact that they had moved in one direction and then the other might throw the hitman off. Their tracks were not as obvious this close to the road. Maybe they had a chance. That was a big maybe. Though his spirits lifted, he knew they were still fighting for survival.

NINETEEN

As she ran, Natasha felt the fatigue leave her muscles. Knowing that they had a chance at getting out alive seemed to have renewed her energy. The memory of the kiss she and Landon had shared, and the power of the connection she felt toward him, still lingered in her mind.

Every once in a while, she glanced up the hill to see the tiny moving light and gauge where the shooter was. He was slowed by having to carry his rifle.

They kept running. She recognized some of the landmarks. A gnarled old tree that arched partway over the road. Their tracks in the snow leading up the hill when they had first escaped the vehicle.

The car came into view. She ran faster. When she looked over her shoulder, she saw the light far down the road. The sniper had tracked them to where they'd come out onto the road. It would take him a while to figure out they'd doubled back this way.

They made it to the car and Landon flung open the trunk. She had a moment of worry that there was no spare in there. He pulled out a tire. She let out the breath she'd been holding. Landon, as well, glanced nervously down the road. The light wasn't visible at all.

Landon pulled his phone out and handed it to her. "If you could turn the flashlight on and angle it so I can see…?"

"Sure, I'll crouch low behind you, so the light won't be visible down the road." She held the phone, and crouched close to Landon while he loosened the lug nuts on the ruined tire and then jacked the car up. He had taken his gloves off to give him more dexterity. He rubbed his hands together.

She peered over his head. Still no sign of the light coming toward them. All the same, her heart was pounding as a sense of urgency spurred her on.

Landon yanked the bad tire off and reached for the good one. She could tell his fingers were getting numb from the cold when he dropped one of the lug nuts in the snow. She shone the light so he could find it. Landon put the good tire on. He rubbed his hands together again.

She pulled off her gloves. "Let me take over. You can warm your hands up. You should be able to tighten the lug nuts with gloves. I'll put them on and make them finger-tight."

He moved out of the way and grabbed his gloves. She quickly put the lug nuts on, the cold sinking into her fingers as she twisted each one as tightly as she could.

After lowering the jack, Landon grabbed the lug wrench. "Go start the car. It's been sitting for a while. I'm sure it will need to warm up."

Natasha handed him his phone back and ran around to the driver's-side door. She sat behind the wheel. They had been in such a hurry to escape, the key was still in the ignition.

She reached for the key, saying a quick prayer that it would start. The car revved to life and she breathed a sigh of relief. She heard the trunk close and then Landon slid into the front passenger's seat.

"Let's go."

"Do you see him?" She craned her neck to look through the back window.

Landon shook his head. "If he's still tracking us, he's turned his flashlight off."

Natasha pressed the gas and the car surged forward. The snow-packed road wound past forests and mountains in the distance. A sign on the road indicated that they were within fifty miles of Anchorage. Almost there.

A car whizzed by them, headed in the other direction.

"That is the first car we have seen since we left that little town," Landon said.

Though the sky had turned a lighter shade of gray, there was still no daylight as they approached the city. Sunrise wouldn't come until 10:00 a.m. The road widened to a paved two-lane. They started to see some houses and buildings as well as more cars on the road.

"Maybe we didn't see the hitman's flashlight behind us on the road because he figured out what we were doing and went back to his car so he could follow us," she said.

"I was thinking that, too," Landon said. "Did the marshal set up a place for you to hole up until we can make contact with him."

"I'm sure he did. We should have a cell signal by now. It would have been texted to your phone." She could see the lights of the city up ahead. "It doesn't feel like Christmas Day to me."

"Me, either."

Landon checked his phone. "You're right. The Mercer Hotel. We are Mr. and Mrs. Johnson. He'll text us where to meet first thing tomorrow." Landon looked up the address of the hotel on his phone and turned on the GPS.

As she wove through the light traffic, it seemed there was very little for them to say to each other. Much of the city looked shut down for the holiday. Seeing the glow of Christmas lights lifted her spirits. The mountains in the distance dusted with snow were beautiful, as well.

Natasha pulled up in front of the office of the hotel. There were some cars parked by rooms but not much sign of any activity. She could see the front desk, but there was no one manning it. "Let's go in together." She turned off the engine and pocketed the keys and they exited the car.

Landon put a protective hand on her back as they entered the lobby. The place appeared deserted. They walked over to the front desk, still not seeing anyone.

"I imagine they have the bare minimum of people working today." Landon tapped the bell on the counter.

She could feel the tension twisting around her torso. Standing there made her feel exposed and vulnerable. She glanced through the floor-to-ceiling window out to where their car was parked.

Landon dinged the bell again.

A woman emerged from a back room. She had dark short hair and looked to be about forty. "So sorry. I hope you haven't been waiting long. What can I do for you?"

Natasha stepped forward. "There should be a reservation for Mr. and Mrs. Johnson."

The woman stepped to one side to look at a computer monitor and then grab a paper from the printer. She tapped the keys. "Yes, here we are. You are in room 213. Just drive around to the side of the building." She pushed the bill toward Natasha.

Natasha laid the cash on the counter.

The clerk turned and grabbed two key cards from a box marked with their room number. She sat the cards on the counter and locked eyes with Natasha. "So unusual to be checking in on Christmas Day."

Natasha's heart fluttered as she tensed. She knew the woman was just making small talk, trying to be friendly, but the less information the desk clerk had, the safer they would be. Just in case the hitman saw their car parked at the hotel or was somehow able to find them and started to ask questions.

Landon stepped forward. "We were delayed in getting here." A true but vague answer.

Natasha's stomach growled. "I don't suppose there's room service, is there?"

"Normally yes, but the restaurant is closed today. There is a convenience store open about three blocks up the street."

Landon grabbed the key cards and handed one to Natasha. He pushed the door open.

This time he sat behind the wheel. "I hadn't thought of it until now, but this car is really distinct. If he's trolling by the hotels and sees it parked, he will know we're here."

"What can we do? There is no place to hide it."

"We can park it far enough away, so he won't connect it with this hotel," Landon said.

"That would mean walking out in the open," she said. "And what if we need to get to it quickly."

"True," he said. "there are not good choices here."

He circled the parking lot that adjoined the hotel finding a space behind a larger van so the car was at least concealed from someone driving by on the the street.

They got out and walked to where their room was. "We'll just have to stay alert. I'll make sure you're safe inside. And I'll go get us something to eat," Landon said.

They walked up the stairs that led to the room. "Stay inside, with the door locked. Don't stand in front of the window. I'll be back as quickly as I can. Don't open the door unless you hear my voice."

Natasha stepped inside, closed the door and clicked the dead bolt into place. After shutting the curtains, she sat on the bed and stared at the wall, listening to the ticking of the clock. The room was clean but most of the décor looked as though it was twenty years out of date. She dared not turn on the television because she didn't want to miss Landon's knock.

She rose from the bed and pulled the curtain back just a sliver to peer outside. Still no sign of another human being. She found the Bible in the nightstand and turned to the Christmas story in Luke. She became so absorbed in the power of the words that when a knock sounded on the door, she jumped.

She waited.

"Natasha, it's me."

She rushed to the door and twisted the dead bolt. He held two grocery bags. "Not much of a selection."

"I'm starving. I could eat almost anything," she said.

He stepped inside. "That's what I have. Almost anything."

She closed and locked the door. After placing the grocery bags down, he sat at the table and started to pull the food out. Christmas candy, some herbal tea packets, microwave popcorn. He held up two boxes. "I thought you might want something warm. Hot dogs and nachos."

"A feast for a king."

"Yes, indeed, a feast for a king. Our king."

She retrieved her coat from the bed where she'd left it when she'd taken it off. She felt in her coat pocket for the carved nativity her grandfather had made. It fit in the palm of her hand. She sat opposite Landon and placed the nativity between them. "This is what matters at Christmas, anyway."

Landon nodded and bowed his head to pray. "God, we thank You for the true gift of Christmas. Your son."

"We thank You for this feast and company to share it with," Natasha said.

"Amen."

Both looked up at the same time. A sense of bitter sweetness washed over her as she gazed into Landon's eyes. She knew from experience that the life you took for granted could be ripped away at any moment. To cling to anything but a faithful God was folly. She reached her hand across the table, placing it on top of his. "I'm going to miss you."

He nodded. His Adam's apple moved up and down.

Unable to bear the sadness she saw in his eyes, Natasha looked away. "Let's dig in."

After she ate the hot dog and half the nachos, her hunger pangs subsided. She heated hot water in the coffeemaker for the herbal tea, which they sipped while taking turns reading the Christmas story from the Bible.

Landon held up the Christmas candy. "Don't forget we have dessert. And the popcorn is for when we watch television. I'm sure there are a ton of Christmas shows airing."

"Let's see what we can find to watch." A sense of satisfaction filled her. She had everything she needed to make Christmas feel like Christmas right here in this room. Too bad it would all be gone tomorrow.

As Landon turned the chair by the table so he could face the television, a sense of finality sank into his bones. In less than twenty-four hours, he'd be saying goodbye to Natasha. He clicked through the channels until he found a show they both remembered from their childhood. Natasha arranged the pillows around her on the bed.

Landon tossed her one of the Christmas candy bars. "Enjoy." The levity he injected into his voice sounded false.

Once the show was over, Natasha yawned. "Are we taking shifts keeping watch?"

He clicked off the television. "I'll take first shift. You get some rest. I'll wake you when I can't keep my eyes open anymore." He scooted the chair back by the window, taking his gun out and placing it on the table.

He pulled the curtain back a sliver and checked the parking lot and the street. There was almost no traffic.

After washing up in the bathroom, Natasha got into bed and pulled the covers up around her. When her breathing changed, he knew that she had fallen asleep.

Landon stayed alert for several hours, checking out the window and pacing the floor. He finally sat back in the chair, feeling his eyelids growing heavy. When his head jerked, he realized he'd nodded off.

Natasha stirred. He stared at the red numbers of the clock on the nightstand. Only a couple more hours and they'd do the handoff. Might as well let her sleep. He catnapped and continued to pace the room.

He woke her an hour before they needed to meet with the marshal. She sat up and smiled then looked at the clock. "You never woke me."

"I figured you needed your sleep," he said. "If you don't mind keeping watch now, I'll take a quick shower and that will wake me up."

She pulled the covers back. "Sure." She placed her feet on the floor and stood.

"The marshal should have texted us by now." He picked up his phone. "Looks like the food court in the Northway Mall. Makes sense. Lots of post-Christmas shoppers around." He couldn't hide the sadness from his voice.

He got up from the chair. She stepped toward him on her way to the window. He reached his hand out and held hers for just a moment. They exchanged a look that was filled with anguish. "We're almost there."

"My new life." Sorrow washed through her words.

He retreated to the bathroom. The lukewarm shower revived him. When he came back in the room, she handed him a paper cup with steam rising from it. "Thought you might want some coffee. I put cream and two sugars in. Hope that's okay."

"That's perfect." He took the cup and sipped, enjoying the warmth and sweetness.

Natasha checked the window one more time. "Still not a lot going on out there."

She sat and finished the coffee she'd prepared for herself. He walked over to the table, set his cup down and picked up his gun so he could return it to the holster.

They both finished their coffee.

In silence, they put on their coats and hats. He kept his gloves in his pocket, knowing he would not be able to shoot a gun with them on.

Landon opened the door and studied the parking lot and the area all around it before stepping to one side. "It looks clear. I'll go first."

She fell into his arms. "Landon, I'm afraid. He was able to track us all the way. Why hasn't he made an appearance? Do you think we were finally able to shake him?"

He relished being able to hold her one more time. His hand brushed over her soft auburn hair. "It seems like he would have come after us by now if he knew where we were. But we can't assume we are in the clear."

She pulled away and gazed into his eyes. "We shouldn't keep Marshal Henderson waiting."

He nodded. They left the hotel room and hurried down to their borrowed vehicle. Landon checked the car and underneath it, as well, for any signs of a bomb or sabotage. The hitman's MO was to shoot at them but that didn't mean he wouldn't change tactics.

Though he could hear the traffic one street over, the hotel parking lot was still all but abandoned. He glanced over his shoulder at the window of their room. Movement in the window of the room above caught his attention. His heartrate accelerated. "Get down."

The shooter had been waiting for them to be in a vulnerable place. Natasha hit the concrete and scuttled to the front bumper of their car. The rifle shot went through the back tire. Same old tactics. Making it impossible to for them to escape in the car.

He crawled around to meet her. "Are you okay?"

She nodded. "He must have tracked us through the marshal. I told you there were snitches."

"This is our chance to take him out. There is only one way in and out of that hotel room." He pulled his phone out. "I'm going to call the police." He pressed in three numbers. "They won't get here in time. We have to be outside that door, ready to catch him when he tries to run." He handed her his gun. "I'll be target practice for him while you sneak up there."

"Landon, no. I don't want to lose you."

He kissed her. "It's the only way." He placed his hand on her cheek.

She nodded. "I don't like it."

"I'll run out. Wait until his focus is on me. He's looking through the scope of a rifle. Move from car to car. He won't see you if you are careful."

She took the gun and put it in her waistband.

Landon glanced up at the window, which was open, though he could not see movement anymore. He picked a car to run toward, knowing he would be exposed for a couple of seconds, and bolted.

The shot came so close to his head, it felt like his

skin was stinging. Staying low, he slipped between two cars and peered at the window. Though he couldn't see Natasha, he had to assume she was on the move.

His heart squeezed tight and he realized his fatal error when he saw movement above the room where he'd glanced. The sniper wasn't in the hotel room above them. He was on the roof.

He feared he had sent Natasha into a deathtrap.

Though the rifle was muffled by some sort of silencer so it wouldn't draw attention, Natasha had picked up on the first shot fired at Landon. She prayed the bullet had not found its target.

She ran from car to car until she was within ten feet of the bottom row of hotel rooms. A second shot was fired. From her hiding place, she lifted her head. She hurried and pressed against the wall of the hotel. The shooter would not see her beneath the overhang created by the balconies above her. She caught a flash of movement in the parking lot. Landon. Another shot was fired and he disappeared around a car.

She raised her head as a realization sank in. The hitman was on the roof. She hurried around to the front of the hotel where she and Landon had checked in. When she entered the lobby, there was no one around. She glanced everywhere. There had to be stairs that led up to the roof.

She ran one way and then the other until she found the door marked "Stairs." She bolted up them, praying that she wasn't too late. Praying that Landon wasn't bleeding to death in the parking lot. The hotel was three stories high. She came to the exit door and pulled her

gun out. She eased the door to the roof open, trying
not to make any noise.

When Natasha looked out, she saw the shooter lying
on his stomach, the rifle poised. In the corner was Marshal Henderson, tied and gagged. That last text message
had probably not even come from him, she realized.

In the distance, she could hear sirens. The hitman
pulled back. In a second he would be packing up his
rifle and preparing to run. He might even shoot the
marshal before he left. This was the moment.

Natasha stepped out. "Step away from the rifle."

His back to her, the man did not move.

"Do it now." She fired a shot, aiming for the man's
hand. He trembled. The shot must have grazed him.

She kept her sights on him as he turned to face her.
She looked into the face of the man who had been trying to kill her for days. He had wild eyes and a scar
across his forehead.

"Too late," he sneered. "Your boyfriend is dead."

Natasha felt like she'd been punched in the stomach, but she held the gun steady. The police had arrived in the parking lot below. The shooter, with his
hands raised, would be fully visible to them. It would
just be a matter of minutes before they were up here.

In her peripheral vision, she could see the marshal
moving, though both his legs and arms had been bound.
She dared not take her eyes off the hitman or let her
guard down, though, inside, she felt like she was col-
lapsing. Landon was dead. He'd given his life for her.

Two police officers arrived on the roof and sprinted
toward the hitman. One pulled out a pair of handcuffs
while the other kept his weapon aimed. Satisfied that
the police had it under control, she ran over to untie

Marshal Henderson. Once he was freed, she gave him a hug. "I am so glad to see you."

The marshal was a man old enough to be her father. "Natasha, so sorry for the dust-up. I didn't expect to be ambushed when I pulled into the hotel parking lot."

"So our meeting place wasn't at the mall?"

The marshal shook his head. "He jumped me and took my phone. I had intended to meet you at this hotel. He must have followed me."

"Yes, we were able to shake him outside of Anchorage."

One police officer remained on the roof while the other escorted the restrained hitman toward the stairs. Marshal nodded toward the remaining officer. "I'll clear things up with the police. You're not going to make a statement. I need to get you out of here to the safe house. I'm impressed you made it all this way. Didn't you say someone was helping you?"

The chasm of pain she had pushed aside hit her now like a sword through her heart. She couldn't even form the words to explain to the marshal all that had happened. She hurried to edge of the roof and looked out at the parking lot. She couldn't see Landon's body anywhere. Her eyes grew moist. She closed her eyes and placed her hand on her chest.

"Come on, Natasha, we need to get going," the marshal said.

She looked all around the cars. "We need to go down to the parking lot." She has to at least make sure Landon's body was taken care of.

A voice came from the other side other roof. "No, you don't."

She whirled around. Landon. Joy surged through

her as she ran to be in his arms. "The shooter said you were dead."

"Well, he lied."

He held her. She breathed in the scent of his neck and rested her cheek against the soft wool of his shirt.

"This must be the man who helped you," said Marshal Henderson, stepping toward them.

Landon pulled away but drew her into a sideways hug. "I'm Landon Defries." He held his free hand toward the marshal. "I'm a state trooper."

"Glad she had your help." After shaking Landon's hand, Marshal Henderson turned to Natasha. "It's still a danger for you to be out in the open like this. We need to go."

Natasha glanced up at Landon as despair overtook her momentary joy. "I know."

Landon looked over to where the man who had chased her across the country was now headed down the stairs. "I need to go help make sure this man stays in custody." He leaned a little closer to her. "I'll make sure they don't know the whole story. Take care of yourself, Natasha."

"Thank you for everything." She felt a tightness through her chest that made it hard to breathe.

He touched her cheek. His features communicated a deep and unspoken tenderness.

This was the way it had to be. They both knew that.

He turned away as tears rimmed her eyes. This was the end of the line for them.

As the marshal escorted her off the rooftop to his waiting car, she was sure she had never known such intense sadness.

TWENTY

Natasha stood on the tarmac of a private airport outside of Anchorage, where a small-engine plane waited to take her to her new life. First to Vancouver and then on a commercial flight to Wyoming.

It was New Year's Eve, but she wouldn't be doing any celebrating.

Marshal Henderson offered her a fatherly hug. "You take care of yourself. I've taken every step to make sure you won't be found again. We are going to find the source of the leak."

She stared at the ground. "I just need to make sure I stay out of the news."

"In addition to the pilot, I've got a law enforcement man aboard for your protection."

Fear fluttered through her. "Are you sure he can be trusted?"

"He's been vetted."

She wasn't so sure about that.

"You'll be fine. Have a good flight," the marshal said. "Take care."

She turned and stepped toward the stairs that led up to the airplane. She carried only a small overnight bag, which contained her new ID and some clothes and toiletries the marshal had gotten for her...and the tiny carved nativity.

Natasha got on the plane. Her protection sat at the back of the plane. The book he was reading hid his face.

Some help he was going to be.

She greeted the pilot and chose a seat right behind the cockpit.

As the pilot prepared for takeoff, her stomach did its usual acrobatic act. She closed her eyes.

A hand covered hers on the armrest.

She opened her eyes, ready to protest such a forward action.

Landon smiled at her. "I know how you hate to fly. Thought you could use some support."

"You're my protection?"

"It's not duty that compels me." He turned to Natasha and she gazed into his eyes. "It's love. Natasha, I can't picture a life without you. What I had back in Little Bear ended when Maggie died. If you'll have me in your new life, I would like to go with you. I'd like to be your husband somewhere down the line."

Natasha couldn't believe what she was hearing. "But you'd be giving up everything."

"But I'd be gaining so much more. I've been working with the marshal all week. My new identity is established, too. We'd be moving to Wyoming as an engaged couple. It's up to you. I can still get off this plane."

She lifted the armrest and fell into his arms. "Of course. I love you, too, and I want to be with you."

Landon kissed her.

The joy Natasha felt was overwhelming. Her life had gone from just surviving to feeling truly, deeply, alive, knowing that she and Landon would grow old together.

The plane lifted off the ground, taking them into a life she knew would be filled with love.

* * * * *

If you enjoyed this book, look for
these other stories by Sharon Dunn:

Undercover Threat
Mountain Captive

Dear Reader,

I hope you enjoyed going on the suspenseful journey with Landon and Natasha. Sometimes when I start a book, while I know the basic plot, I'm not sure what spiritual truth will emerge. That was the case with this book. The characters' life circumstances usually indicate what that truth is. Natasha has suffered many losses in her life. Her husband being shot in the line of duty, and then her being torn from her job, friends and family when she had to enter WITSEC. Landon, as well, has lost the woman he loved. Natasha says more than once that the trauma she has been through has made her realize that the only constant in any life is God and His love. Such a hard truth in so many ways. No one wants to go through trouble and pain. We like being comfortable. Yet, it is the losses that have made me depend on God more, and that have given me a deeper compassion for others. God is with us always and He is faithful.

Take care,
Sharon Dunn

"Mom!"

That had been a child's cry. State police officer Patrick Sanders glanced across the open desert at the base of a mountain.

Had he found what he was looking for?

Tucker sniffed, nose turned to the breeze.

Patrick's K-9 partner, an Airedale terrier he'd gotten from a shelter as a puppy and trained, scented the wind. His body stiffened and he leaned forward. As an air-scent dog, Tucker didn't need a trail to follow. He could catch the scent he was looking for on the wind or, in this case, the winter breeze rolling over the mountain.

Patrick's mountains, the place he'd grown up. Until right before his high school graduation when his mom had packed them up and fled town. They'd lost their home and everything they'd had there.

Including the girl Patrick had loved.

He heard another cry. Stifled by something—it was hard to hear as it drifted across so much open terrain.

He and his K-9 had been dispatched to find Jennie and her son, Nathan. A friend had reported them missing yesterday, and the sheriff wasted no time at all calling for a search and rescue team from state police.

The dog had caught a scent and was closing in.

As a terrier, it was about the challenge. Tucker had proved to be both prey-driven, like fetching a ball, and food-driven, like a nice piece of chicken, when he felt like it.

Right now the dog had to find Jennie and the boy so Patrick could transport them to safety. Then he intended to get out of town again. Back to his life in Albuquerque and studying for the sergeant's exam.

Tucker tugged harder on the leash; a signal the scent was stronger. He was closing in. Patrick's night of searching for the missing woman and her child would soon be over.

Tucker rounded a sagebrush and sat.

"Good boy. Yes, you are." Patrick let the leash slacken a little. He circled his dog and found Jennie lying on the ground.

"Jennie."

She stirred. Her eyes flashed open and she cried out. *"We need to find Nate."*

Don't miss
Desert Rescue *by Lisa Phillips,*
available wherever Love Inspired Suspense books and ebooks are sold.

LoveInspired.com

LISEXP1220